Praise for *Lords of*

"Jackson Ellis' *Lords of St. Thomas* is the dramatic story of the beleaguered Lord family, forced off their land by the creation of Lake Mead. At the heart of the book are the patriarch Henry Lord, who refuses to leave his doomed home, and town, and his young grandson and namesake. *Lords of St. Thomas* is both a terrific coming-of-age story and an exact and haunting evocation of a bygone time and place. What's more, it's a great read. I loved every page."

—HOWARD FRANK MOSHER, author of
Where the Rivers Flow North and *Disappearances*

"Jackson Ellis' totally transporting coming-of-age tale takes you to a world or scorching sun, unstoppable storms, and acutely observed heartache. *Lords of St. Thomas* manages to exist on two planes, succeeding both as compelling historical fiction about one man's steadfast refusal to give in to the rising tide of modernity, and as a beautifully elegiac tribute to lives (and a way of life) now lost. A fascinating, fast-paced, and frequently lovely examination of human struggle in the face of constant change."

—JEREMY ROBERT JOHNSON, author of
Entropy in Bloom and *Skullcrack City*

"With *Lords of St. Thomas* Jackson Ellis has written a book that is part historic, part environmental, part familial, and always compelling. Ellis draws us deep into the lives of the Lord family as they face the loss of their home, their community, their way of life, and even themselves to the rising waters of Lake Mead. And we readers are sucked along as the family wrestles with the decision to leave or stay while fighting to survive. It's a story that forces the reader to keep reading, one page after the next, to see what becomes of historic St. Thomas—and what becomes of the Lords."

—SEAN PRENTISS, author of *Finding Abbey: The Search
for Edward Abbey and His Hidden Desert Grave*

"*Lords of St. Thomas* is a timely, tender, thought-provoking family saga about the importance of keeping promises—no matter how long they take to fulfill. With a playful touch, Jackson Ellis has gifted us with a daring story rich in premise and intrigue with just the right amount of suspense and pathos."

—NATHANIEL G. MOORE, author of
Savage 1986-2011 and *Jettison*

LORDS OF
ST. THOMAS

GREEN WRITERS PRESS *Brattleboro, Vermont*

LORDS OF ST. THOMAS

A NOVEL

Jackson Ellis

Printed in the United States

10 9 8 7 6 5 4 3

Green Writers Press is a Vermont-based publisher whose mission
is to spread a message of hope and renewal through the words and
images we publish. Throughout we will adhere to our commitment to
preserving and protecting the natural resources of the earth. To that
end, a percentage of our proceeds will be donated to environmental
activist groups. Green Writers Press gratefully acknowledges support
from individual donors, friends, and readers to help support the
environment and our publishing initiative.

GReen
wRiTers
p r e s s

Giving Voice to Writers & Artists Who Will Make the World a Better Place
Green Writers Press | Brattleboro, Vermont • www.greenwriterspress.com

ISBN: 978-0-9990766-8-2

Cover art and design by Nathaniel Pollard | hello@nathanpollard.com

PRINTED ON PAPER WITH PULP THAT COMES FROM FSC-CERTIFIED FORESTS, MANAGED FORESTS
THAT GUARANTEE RESPONSIBLE ENVIRONMENTAL, SOCIAL, AND ECONOMIC PRACTICES.

TO MY FAMILY

ACKNOWLEDGMENTS

Love and gratitude to my wife, Nathalia, my daughter, Sophie, my parents, Tom and Holly, and my brother, Asher. Thanks to early readers who offered feedback and support, including Aunt Barbara and Jimmy Pappas, Heela Naqshband and Shahab Zargari, Douglas Novielli, Raegan Butcher, Heather and Jason Schofner, Kevin Munley, and my mom, wife, and brother. Extra special thanks to Heela and the University of Nevada, Las Vegas Libraries Digital Collections. Thank you Nate Pollard for designing a beautiful book cover and for all the years of creative collaboration and friendship. Thank you Sean Prentiss, Nathaniel G. Moore, and Jeremy Robert Johnson for your enthusiasm and kind words. Thank you editors John K. Tiholiz and Josh Bovee for your keen insights and crucial attention to detail, and for helping me see this book through to completion. A huge thank you to Dede Cummings and everyone at Green Writers Press for believing in me and for running a wonderful publishing house. And thank you Howard Frank Mosher for the invaluable advice and encouragement you gave not just to me, but to countless writers. You are greatly missed.

If you'd like to learn more about the true history of St. Thomas, Nevada, and Hugh Lord (the real-life inspiration for Henry Lord), I highly recommend Aaron McArthur's excellent, thoroughly researched book, *St. Thomas, Nevada: A History Uncovered* (University of Nevada Press, 2013). And if you ever find yourself in the Las Vegas area, head northeast from Vegas about 90 minutes to seek out the ruins of St. Thomas, now part of the Lake Mead National Recreation Area. Bring plenty of water.

LORDS OF
ST. THOMAS

❖

"Wake up, boy. It's time to go. We have to get out of here now."

I'm not sure whether it was the foul scent filling my nostrils that woke me, or if it was my grandfather's booming voice, but I immediately became aware of both. Grandpa stood over me, fully dressed, beside my bed. As always, his overalls and thick, calloused hands reeked of engine oil and gasoline. However, on this morning, the smell was much stronger than usual.

Dizzy from noxious fumes, I stumbled down the stairs and splashed through our flooded living room, cool water lapping at the tops of my ankles. Moments later, we shoved off from the porch, where my grandfather had anchored the dinghy the night before. Circling behind the house, he struck a match and set the flame to the entire book. Then, with a flick of his wrist, he flung the burning matchbook through the open kitchen window.

It was June 11, 1938—a clear, dry day like so many others in the parched Mojave Desert. The rising sun roasted us like fish in a skillet as we floated beneath the steel blue sky through the Moapa Valley in an aluminum rowboat.

In my lap I clutched a Gladstone bag containing little more than a few changes of clothes. My grandfather sat with his back to me, leaning into the oars, breathing hard through his nose. As the two-story house shrank on the horizon, flames appeared to burst forth from the water and feast on the clapboards. The house turned black beneath the fire.

When we pulled ashore on the crumbly, ashen slope of the plateau northwest of town I looked back one last time to see the structure cave in and collapse into the encroaching waters of Lake Mead, which quickly extinguished the burning ruins and belched skyward a thick black plume of smoke. From more than a third of a mile away I could hear the wreck hiss and sizzle.

In the early autumn, we returned to the same plateau we'd landed at the base of months earlier, though now the water nearly reached the top. We surveyed what was once our town but saw only the tips of a few chimneys and roof peaks poking through the surface of the lake and the tops of the tallest remaining trees shedding their leaves for the final time as they slowly submerged.

The old man squeezed my shoulders as we reminisced, mourning for all that we had lost. He would never go back. It would take me sixty-four years to return in search of what I'd left behind.

PART ONE

PART ONE

1.

Colorful lights and decorations were strung all through the dimly lit Sahara Saloon. Christmas was still two and a half weeks away, but everyone—from the bartenders to the regulars to the lost tourists who staggered in every now and then—already seemed to be full of holiday cheer. Even the chain-smoking drunks who never left their posts at the slots were in pretty decent spirits.

It was an old and rank-smelling dive, but I'd grown attached to it. Like most bars in Las Vegas, it stayed open twenty-four hours a day. But it set itself apart by having its own greasy spoon in the back. No matter the hour, I could always grab a coffee and a pancake or a quick, cheap pint—whatever I was in the mood for.

Even if I didn't like it I'd still probably frequent it—the saloon was the closest eatery to my winter home, a flimsy little two-room ranch house a couple blocks from the intersection of Sahara Avenue and the Boulder Highway. At the age of seventy-six, I wasn't too interested in driving long distances if I didn't have to. Convenience and comfort become chief priorities once you reach old age.

I sat down alone at a small table for two. "Good morning, Mr. Lord," said Louis, a jack-of-all-trades server and cook. His rumbly voice, heavy with nicotine, made him sound years older than his actual age of thirty-five. "Here for the usual?"

"Not too hungry this morning, Louis. I'll just take some toast and potatoes." Then I turned over the upside-down coffee mug on top of the paper placemat. "But first, how about a shot of caffeine to make sure my heart doesn't stop? You've gotta help keep me alive so I can make it to Christmas."

He laughed and poured out a cup of coffee from the pot he already had in his hand. "This should be enough to get you through at least noon, Henry."

I was in a good mood myself, and it wasn't just because of the upbeat yuletide carols on the radio that had wormed their way into my head. In just a matter of days I'd be bound for Seattle, flying out of McCarran Airport to be with my children and grandkids for a three-week holiday vacation. Considering that we were spread across the country the rest of the year, it would be a rare reunion with the whole family.

Within minutes, Louis delivered my food. Just as I was about to take my first bite of home fries, Charlie Snyder, another regular, spun around on his stool, crinkling the ancient duct tape that held together the cracked red vinyl of the seat cushion. In his hands he held aloft a section of newspaper, which he did not look up from.

"Say, Hank," he called to me. "That place you're from that you told us about. St. Thomas, right?"

I put down my fork and raised my head. "Yes, that's the one. Why do you mention it?"

He took a few steps over to my table and held the folded newspaper in front of my nose.

"Look at this."

"Drought Exposes St. Thomas," announced the "Living" section headline of the December 8, 2002 edition of the *Las Vegas Review-Journal*.

Not many living people have seen the settlement of St. Thomas, it began. *The town has been underwater since 1938, when the Hoover Dam backed up the Colorado River to create Lake Mead. But now, receding waters, brought on by severe drought, have allowed the town to surface.*

"So that's the place, eh?" said Charlie, awaiting my reaction.

If the ghosts of Elvis Presley and Frank Sinatra had sat down and invited me out for a drink at the Copa Room I couldn't have been more shocked. I only nodded my head silently for a moment and pointed at the photo accompanying the article.

"That's the place, Chuck," I finally whispered. "And that, right there, front and center in the photo? That's what's left of the house I grew up in."

Sticking a few feet out of the desert floor, bleached by water, sun, and time, was the concrete foundation of the Lord homestead. And there, near the ground, perfectly unobstructed, was the gaping opening of the foundation window, inviting me back into the black confines of the crawlspace.

2.

The small town of St. Thomas, Nevada, sat along the edge of the Muddy River near its confluence with the Virgin River, twenty miles north of the drainage into the Colorado. It was sweltering, isolated, lonely, dusty, and primitive—nearly fifty miles from Las Vegas, and far out of sight of the nearby ranching community of Overton, located on higher ground to the northwest.

I was born there on August 20, 1926, at the home of my mother and father and my father's father, for whom I was named. Though life can be difficult to sustain under the hard desert sun, we had the luxury of water flowing by in our backyards, more than enough to keep full the cisterns of several hundred townspeople.

The ignorance of childhood can be a wonderful thing. At the time I did not realize that I had been born into a doomed home in a doomed town. For that I am thankful.

St. Thomas was my entire world during those early years. I would stand on my bed on the second floor of our house and peer out the window over the hamlet, a mere six blocks of streets lined with grassy yards, low fences, and tall cottonwoods and fig trees. I didn't understand that the massive schoolhouse across the street, where my mother once taught, was shuttered for good, and that I'd never attend it. I could never have predicted that Hannig's Ice Cream Parlor would serve me my last cone before I learned to count past ten, or that the fields of barley and the shady pear orchards that lined the runnels would be abandoned first to dry up and then to drown.

The nearby Nutter Store had been shuttered since I could remember, which meant we had to cross town to shop at Gentry's General Store for groceries. Sellar's Café and Pool Hall—the only place in town where you could get together with friends after a long day of work—shut down in the early '30s too.

But I was never bothered and never bored. My father began to teach me to play baseball as soon as I could throw a ball, and we spent every possible morning and evening (to avoid the intense midday heat) in the abandoned schoolyard playing catch. I learned to field ground balls and pop flies, and occasionally peppered the brick façade of the old school with a ball when my father wasn't around. It never struck me as odd that there were practically no other children around to play with.

My grandpa, Henry Lord, had lived in the valley for most of his life—all of it that he could remember—having relocated as an infant with his parents in 1869. My great-grandparents had been commanded by Brigham Young to relocate from Salt Lake City as part of the original mission, and when the Latter-day Saints abandoned St. Thomas en masse a mere two years later—having learned that the town sat in the State of Nevada, *not* in Utah as originally believed—my forebears were the only founding residents to stay put. No longer among fellow Saints, but rather native Paiutes, miners, and drunken outlaws who swarmed in to populate the vacated town, they became apostates and were excommunicated by the LDS disciplinary council.

Regardless of the church's actions, my grandfather was raised in the Mormon faith. His reverence for both his home and the church was reflected in the name he gave my father, Thomas, born in 1900 and named for the founder of the town, Thomas Smith. My mother, Ellen, was born in St. Thomas in 1906, and at the age of twenty married my father in the same year she became a schoolteacher. It was a job she'd hold for only five short years.

From a young age, Grandpa worked as a farmhand in the irrigated fields southeast of town, and also was instrumental in bringing the San Pedro Railroad spur line into St. Thomas. Later he would run the town's first—and only—automobile garage, situated on the Arrowhead Trail highway, US Route 91, serving tourists and auto club members traveling from Los Angeles to Utah and back again.

Over the many years he'd lived in his home, Grandpa, along with my mother, had collected a massive library of books. At night I would sit in the parlor with them under the dim light of the oil lanterns mounted on the wall above the sofa, and together they taught me to read at the age of four. By the time I began my mother's homeschooling lessons, I was reading Rudyard Kipling and Lewis Carroll for enjoyment.

It was an idyllic childhood in the oddest place, an oasis in a vast desert valley, and the reality that this would not last forever was lost on me. So too were the reasons why my dad and my grandpa rarely spoke after the day my parents returned from a five-day trip to Boulder City.

The silent feud became normal to me, and I didn't think twice when they would pass by each other in the home without exchanging pleasantries or even a glance, despite both lavishing attention and affection on me. Meals were often eaten in silence, and during our weekend walks to Gentry's, only one and not the other would accompany my mother and me.

3.

T HOUGH THE RIFT between father and son
formed in 1933, it could actually be traced
back earlier. In 1928, Congress approved a
plan to build the Boulder Dam at a narrow section
of the Colorado River in Black Canyon. And on
December 21 of that year, four months after my second birthday, President Calvin Coolidge signed the
Boulder Canyon Project Act. The death knell rang for
the small settlement situated just seventy miles to the
north.

"The damn dam bill passed," became the common
cry of despair around town. The federal government
purchased all the surrounding land. Officials began
to come around, promising to pay a fair market price
for homes while urging townspeople to relocate to
Overton, Logandale, Las Vegas, and Boulder City. St.

Thomas was a mortal village, terminally wounded. A
dead town walking.

"It was crippling," my grandpa said years later, his
face somber with the memory. "It was Christmastime,
but we were miserable—me, your dad, your mom—
everyone in town. We had lost everything.

"So I decided to fight it."

•

When the school closed and was subsequently abandoned, my father swiped two beautiful iron-and-oak
desks from my mother's classroom—one sat in our
home's parlor, where I'd sit for my homeschooling
lessons, and the other stayed in the rear corner of
Grandpa's small auto shop. The lift-top desk was a
perfect place to sock away Lincoln Logs and comic
books. It wasn't unusual for midday temperatures in
the Mojave to soar to well over a hundred degrees,
and I enjoyed passing the sweltering days in the dark,
cool concrete building while my father and grandfather tinkered on the occasional customer's car.

One early summer day, I was sitting in the back
of the building, playing by myself as I almost always
did. My father and grandfather stood grimly near
the wide-open garage door, surveying the still, dusty
street. Suddenly, coming from the west, we heard the
welcome noise of an approaching auto, slowly rumbling down the bumpy road rutted by the majority
traffic of horses and carts. A fancy, slate-colored
car pulled up in front of the garage sidelong to the
entrance, not facing inward like most drivers who

needed a repair, and out stepped a well-dressed man who seemed entirely out of place in such heat.

He wore a gray woolen vest and suit coat over a buttoned shirt and plaid cravat. His wrinkled face was beet red, and sweat streaked down the creases of his face like a hot waterfall. Curious, I wandered up to the entrance of the garage and stood behind my father, peering around his waist at the visitor.

"Good afternoon, Mr. Lord," he said, extending his arm and offering a flushed hand to my grandfather.

"Afternoon, yourself," he replied, taking the man's hand in a crushing grip and shaking vigorously, as if he were trying to wrench the man's shoulder from its socket. My dad stood back and folded his arms on his chest.

The man winced and slowly retracted his hand. He placed it against his suit coat, awkwardly trying to find a natural-looking place for his tender fingers to rest. "Well, yes, anyway," he said, and cleared his throat, pausing awkwardly. "How is business faring?" he asked, craning his neck, peeking into the empty garage. "I wouldn't believe it to be *terribly* busy these days."

"Business is fine," Grandpa replied, his voice booming off the walls of the building.

"Great. Well, why don't we all have a seat?" said the man, motioning into the garage as if we were the guests.

"The answer is still 'no,'" said my grandfather, cutting him off. "We haven't changed our mind. We're not selling, we're not leaving, and we're not taking your money."

"Henry, we are offering you a fair price for your property—for all of your property, and we will help you relocate your home and your business if you'd just accept the fact that the dam is going to be built, and you're going to be left high and—"

He stuttered and failed to finish his sentence, but the point had been made, and his demeanor had shifted—the politeness fell away like shed snakeskin.

"High and what now?" Grandpa pressed. "If you were going to say what I think you were going to say, then I suppose we're finally getting what we want."

"Two thousand dollars for your home, and twelve hundred for your garage, Mr. Lord," replied the official. "Nearly double our original offer. We will help you to purchase new property, and we will assist in your relocation. It is the very best we can offer."

My grandpa stared directly into his eyes and said nothing. My father shifted on his feet and glanced nervously, back and forth between the two men. He opened his mouth as if to say something, but remained silent.

"They started pouring concrete this week. You'd be a fool not to accept this offer!" said the old man in the suit, his irritation at my grandpa's obstinacy growing with every second.

"Are you going to pay for the shade?" my grandfather asked.

The man from the government stood in befuddled silence for a moment. "Beg your pardon?"

"I asked, 'Are you going to pay for the shade?' I mean, here in the valley, on a day as hot as this, the shade of these old trees my father planted all around our property is, well, priceless. So I ask again, can you pay me for the shade?"

"That's a preposterous proposal, Henry, and you know for a fact that we cannot *pay* you for something as *intangible* as the shade, valuable as it may be to you now—"

"Then there's no deal." My grandfather shook his head and sighed. I remember the feeling of his thick, heavy hand palming my head as if it were a small melon as he roughly tousled my hair. Then he turned and walked back into the garage without a word, leaving my dad and me at the entrance.

The government official turned and stomped back to his car, entirely ignoring my father. Once seated, he leaned out the window and shouted, "Move out, or we're going to flood you out! The choice is yours, Henry." As he drove away, my father and I stood in the doorway, watching his car rumble down the nearly empty street, spewing a thin plume of reddish dust into the air.

"This isn't some here-today-gone-tomorrow gold rush town," Grandpa grumbled. "We don't live in *shacks*. These are real homes and businesses. They can't force us out."

Of course, by this time, people had been leaving St. Thomas in droves. Half of the small town was deserted, and it seemed that each week another family or business would vacate. Bare concrete slabs surrounded by dead grass and empty flowerbeds marked the spots where entire houses had once stood, having been dismantled and fully rebuilt in neighboring Overton or Logandale. Other structures were simply deserted.

And it seemed as though my grandfather were blind to it all.

"Dad, I was thinking," said my father in a hushed voice. "Maybe we should stop trying to fight this and just take the money. We can rebuild the house and the garage—start making money again. I don't think we're going to win this one."

Grandpa stared at him through slit eyes, a look of pure revulsion. Then he picked up a broom and began to sweep the floor, though it was already cleaner than any auto shop floor should be.

"You heard what he said. They started pouring concrete this week. It's going to happen, no matter what we do."

My grandfather turned his back and swept harder, proclaiming, "The water will never make it this far."

"I'm going to walk home," said my dad.

"Work day's not over yet," came the reply.

"Come and get me when business picks up." He put on his hat and walked out into the blistering heat of midafternoon. I retreated to my desk in the dark corner and pulled some toy cars out of the cubby, and listened to the sound of corn broom bristles scraping clean, bare concrete.

4.

THAT EVENING, when the sun had settled low in the sky and the mock orange and cottonwood trees cast long shadows down the street, my grandpa took me by the hand and led me home. The streets and the sidewalks were vacant, but I remember hearing the clatter of a single truck rumbling in the distance behind us, heading west out of town.

When we got home, we found that it had been ours. The truck was missing, and once inside, we realized that both of my parents were gone too. Cans and bags and bottles of supplies from Gentry's had been hastily scattered near the dining table and pantry, along with a note that I found under a soup can. It simply read, *Gone to Boulder City. Back soon.*

I handed it to my grandfather, and he crumpled the note in his fist and shoved it into the hip pocket of his overalls. Then he picked up a bag of groceries and said, "Hey, boy, how about you help me put these away? Then we'll put on our boots and go down to the river."

"Why did Mom and Dad leave?" I asked. "They had to go do something, I suppose. Don't you worry. They'll be back soon."

I passed him cans and bottles, one at a time, and he stacked them on the pantry shelves. Then we pulled on our boots and walked outside just as the sun began to drop behind the mesas on the horizon. In the balmy twilight we headed to the Muddy River on the eastern edge of town. We passed through recently vacated farmlands, kicking up puffs of dust where formerly rich, irrigated soil had dried and grape arbors had given way to tangled sprouts of creosote.

The river no longer rushed with springtime runoff, and a small crumbling bank had formed where the high-water mark had been. We skidded down, causing miniature avalanches over the mouths of rattlesnake and tarantula dens. At the riverside we picked up smooth pebbles, still warm from the daylong sun bake, and plunked them into the middle of the channel's dark green waters. Sunlight still lingered high overhead on the summit of Virgin Peak; its heavily forested slopes bore a stark contrast to the dry land below. After some time, my grandpa stopped hurling rocks and sat down behind me.

"Keep throwing 'em," he encouraged. "If you throw enough, you'll fill it up and we can stop the river here. Then we can move on to the Colorado!"

He laughed quick and loud, but I believed what he said. I didn't know why Grandpa wanted the river to stop, but I believed that maybe it had something to do with my mom and dad's leaving home—so I threw faster, harder, with great purpose. Maybe if I could dam it up before bedtime, my folks might come back right away.

The rocky cliffs watched us below in the dying valley and blew down gentle, soothing winds while darkness settled, the only sounds the intermittent *kerplunks* of my pebbles and the whispering waters which seemed to be saying something, only I couldn't understand it, and my grandfather refused to listen.

5.

FIVE DAYS LATER, on a Saturday afternoon, I was sitting with a picture book in the living room when I heard a truck engine groaning in the yard. I ran to the window and pressed my nose against the hot pane to peer out into the bright sunlight. My mother and father stepped out and hoisted their luggage from the bed of the truck. Big smiles lit up their tired-looking faces when they saw me through the glass.

I ran to the door and out onto the farmer's porch, and they dropped their trunks on the ground to rush toward me. They knelt down at the top of the steps, one on each side, and hugged me and kissed my cheeks.

"Hey, buckaroo! How's my man?" asked my dad.

"Oh, honey, we missed you so much!" said my mom. "Did you behave for Grandpa?"

I remember crying as soon as I heard my mother's voice. Overwhelmed with relief that they'd returned for me, I held them tight around their necks, burying my wet face in their collars as they picked me up and passed me back and forth. Though my grandfather had told me repeatedly that they'd come back, I couldn't know for sure whether he was telling the truth—the anger and sadness he'd attempted to suppress during the previous week had been apparent even to a young child like me; it floated through the garage and about the house like the dust that blew in through the screen windows. I could feel it all around me even if I couldn't see it.

With my mother following, my father carried me into the house in one arm, his trunk in his other hand, and he set us both down gently on the parlor floor near the foot of the staircase.

He knelt down to unlatch the trunk and then suddenly froze when he realized Grandpa had appeared in the darkened entryway that led to the dining room.

"Hi, Dad," he said quietly. Immediately, my mother lowered her head and gripped my hand, pulling me behind her as she ascended the stairs. At the top she let go, and we both sat down behind the railing, just out of sight of the men below. I crawled back to the top step and peered down between the wooden balusters.

"I'm afraid to ask, Thomas," said my grandfather, "but I'm afraid I already know. Where've you been?" His voice had a somber timbre that I'd never heard before.

"Boulder City." My dad's reply was flat, but he somehow sounded stronger than my grandpa.

"I know that. How come?"

"Because, Dad, unlike you, I'm thinking about the future. Because I have a kid and a wife I have to think about. I'm not happy about any of this, but I have to do what's best." His voice was even and strong, though he continued to kneel. He appeared to be genuflecting before my grandfather as he opened his trunk and rifled through the neatly folded clothes.

"All right, then. So, tell me, what is *best*?"

My father found what he was looking for. From his trunk he removed a handsome brown woolen work shirt. He unfolded it and stood up to display it. It had a stiff collar and thick buttons, and sewn to the breast were the words "Six Companies"—the corporation tasked with building the Boulder Dam.

"They need more men, so I'm starting on Monday. I'll be starting out on a crew of high scalers. Clearing rock and hauling it out of the canyon."

My grandfather never even glanced at the uniform shirt held aloft by my father. His eyelids twitched, the corners of his downturned mouth quivered, and his forehead crumpled as he kept his eyes fixed on his son.

"It pays well. Really well," continued my dad. "Seventy cents an hour, which means I'll be able to start saving some money for Little Henry. The garage isn't making too much these days, and—"

He paused and finally relaxed his arms, lowering the shirt.

"And I'll be able to buy a house, seeing as how you won't take the government money."

My grandpa's features softened. His frown relaxed, his brow unfurrowed, and his eyes suddenly looked sad and wet.

"Son, you know I've got some money saved away—" he started.

"Dad, that's *your* money. The garage is *your* business. But this is my family, and I can't stay indebted to you—to your money, or to your home. If you won't leave with us, then we'll have to leave without you, and I'll have to buy my own place."

"But what's mine is yours, and your family's," the old man countered. "This was my land and now it's *ours*. Someday it will be yours. You have to hold on to it. When you get a chunk of land like we've got here, you've got to hang on to it. And when someone tries to take it from you, you've got to fight. You've got to fight and scrap and claw to hang on and never let anyone take what's yours, no matter who it is."

"No one's taking anything from you that can't be replaced, Dad," my father snapped, and the words seemed to knock the wind ever further out of my grandpa; he staggered backward a step as though he'd taken a body blow. "And they're not taking it for free. They're offering you money that you won't take. You won't ever accept help."

"Shoving me out the door of my own house is help? Telling me I can't stay where I want to stay in a home that I bought and paid for and been living in most of my life is help? Destroying my business and forcing my neighbors out is *help*?"

"No, Dad, but the money they're offering would be a great help," my father replied. "And you're about the only one who won't take it. No one is happy about this. I'm not, and Ellen's not, and nobody in this damned town is happy, but we're doing our best to accept it and make the best of our lousy situation. There are other places to work and live out there, and I aim to land on higher ground where the water won't reach." Wearily, he shuffled over to the banister and leaned his full weight on it. I scooted away from the railing at the top, farther into the shadows of the hallway where I wouldn't be seen.

"That's the problem with you, boy." My grandfather began to slowly pace. His boots clomped and the wood floorboards creaked. "You believe anything anybody tells you. That dam is seventy miles away. No way in *Hell* is that water going to reach us here at the north end of town."

With that, my dad reenergized. He pushed himself from the railing and spun toward his father, pointing and wagging a finger. "You're a smart man, Dad, but you don't know everything! You want to tell me you know better than all those planners and engineers and dam builders? You know better than all the other people in town who've left and plan to leave? Do you *really* think the government is offering you cold, hard cash for your land because we *won't* be flooded out?"

Grandpa's face no longer appeared gentle or sympathetic. The vulnerability was gone, and he once again hardened his face into a crooked, crunched scowl.

"So you're going to go ahead and leave your old man. You're going to feed the hand that bites you."

"It's 'bite the hand that feeds you,' Dad."

"No, it's not—not this time. We've got a lot against us here, living in the middle of nowhere in a desert hot as blazes where neither man nor beast should survive—but we've made it work. And now we've got an enemy nipping at us like dogs, chasing us away, and you're giving them consent. And now you're going to work for them. You're feeding the dogs."

He paused and cast his eyes downward.

"Well, go ahead. But I'm not wrong. You'll wish you'd listened to me, and you'll feel like a fool. Go ahead and take that government job."

"I already have." My dad turned and began walking up the stairs. At the top he bent down where my mother still sat on the floor and kissed the top of her head. Streaks of silent tears dried on her cheeks. Then he grabbed our baseball mitts, picked me up, and carried me outdoors to play in the shady schoolyard.

I'm not sure, but it may have been the last time either man spoke to the other.

6.

AFTER THAT, my father's presence at home became increasingly rare. For up to weeks at a time he'd be away, returning on the occasional Saturday just to turn around and leave again the following afternoon. The days working at the dam were long and strenuous, and the ocean of desert between St. Thomas and Boulder City proved to be too vast to traverse for a midweek evening visit.

My parents and my grandfather were the only people in my life, and now they were divided by both distance and irreconcilable animosity. My grandfather and mother both seemed subtly changed; quiet people by nature, they seemed to speak even less to each other and to me, and their tempers flared more easily.

When he did visit, my father too seemed changed. Even then I understood that sixty hours of backbreaking labor per week would do that to a man. Whenever he arrived at the door, the thin smile on his face communicated the blend of joy and sorrow percolating behind his furrowed brow. He spoke without moving his lips.

His skin had become darker, rougher, and as wrinkled as an elephant's, and his eyes were entirely bloodshot, as though the whites had been permanently burnt by the sun. While he remained as cheerful as ever when we were together, he moved slower, belabored by fatigue.

When we played baseball in the old schoolyard, he would often try to take a seat. He'd never done that before, even on the most brutally hot days.

"I need a rest, pal," he would say as he slowly knelt down in the dry, dead grass beneath a cottonwood. "How about I take a seat over here and watch you for a bit? Throw the ball off the wall and show me how well you can field a ground ball."

"But I play by myself all the time," I'd argue, rubbing my fingers on the scuffed leather surface of the ball. The brick walls of the school building had shredded its cover and split open the seams. "I want to play catch with you. Can't you throw me some grounders? And maybe some pop flies?"

He'd slowly stand, wincing at the sharp pains in his lower back and knees. Then he'd offer a smile, put out his glove, and I'd fire the ball to him. "You've got a great arm," he'd say. He would roll and loft the ball to me until it was nearly dark. Sometimes my mom would come over to sit and watch. Sometimes I'd see my grandfather watching too from a distance, leaning on the old post-and-rail wooden fence.

7.

MIDSUMMER HEAT in the Nevada desert is torturous, as if the hand of God were holding a magnifying glass over the parched crust of the Earth to torch ants that dared to venture away from their colony. Even for the animals and plants that know no other way of life, the months slowly roll by, a brutal endurance challenge.

Humans have it no easier, and every July and August I tended to pass most of the days indoors. Of course, when my dad arrived to celebrate my birthday on the third weekend of August 1934—the first time he'd visited in a month—I pounced on him outside, ready to grab the ball and gloves despite the triple-digit temperature.

"It's too hot to play right now," he said. "But grab your ball anyway. Quick, get it!"

I leaped up the front steps and burst through the front door. I grabbed the ball out of my glove, which was sitting on the floor where I'd placed it that morning, and returned with it outside. It was a tragic, pathetic baseball. Bluish-gray yarn burst through the tattered leather, which threatened to fall off at any moment. Months of ricochets off the brick wall had all but destroyed it.

"Well, look at that thing," Dad exclaimed as he plucked it from my fingers. "How about this: for your birthday, I'll trade you that old ragged ball for a whole bunch of new ones." He reached into the cab of the truck and pulled out a paper bag. Inside were a half-dozen brand new baseballs. I picked up one and turned it in my fingers, amazed at the smooth, brilliant white leather and the tight red seams. I'd grown so accustomed to my ball that I'd forgotten how a fresh store-bought baseball looked and felt.

"What do you think? Think those will last you a while?"

"Yep," I said, pleased with the haul, "and if you come home more, then I won't have to go ruining them on the wall!"

"I'll do what I can, pal," he said, squinting at me. "Say, it's pretty hot out here. Why don't we go inside so I can say hello to your mom? I have something else I want to show you in a little while."

•

Upstairs, my dad greeted my mom behind the closed doors of their bedroom while I waited downstairs in the kitchen, drinking lemonade and eating a bowl of the ice cream my grandfather had picked up at Gentry's. He sat at the table quietly sipping lemonade, watching me wolf down the special birthday treat before it completely melted into soup. Soon I was a sticky mess, my fingers and cheeks coated with chocolate.

As I finished the last spoonful, my dad entered the kitchen with our gloves and a bright white baseball. I jumped out of my seat, but before I could take a step toward him my grandfather snapped, "You're not leaving just yet. You know where that bowl goes. I'm not picking up after you."

I turned around, grabbed the bowl, and brought it up to the sink.

"Hey, Dad," said my father under his breath.

"And wash your hands and face too," said Grandpa, ignoring my dad's greeting as he slowly arose and walked out the back door. "The cistern's getting low on water, so don't use too much. Never take water for granted in the desert."

•

After I washed up, we went outside and started to cross the street toward the schoolyard—but then my dad pulled me by the hand and we doubled back to his pickup truck, where he quietly opened the door and placed our gloves and the ball inside.

"Hey," I protested, "I thought we were going to play!"

"Quiet," he whispered. "We'll play later. It's too hot anyway. Right now I have something else to show you."

Sitting on the passenger side floor of the truck's cab was a lantern, which he lit—odd, considering that the sunlight was practically blinding unless you stood in the shade. Then he stuffed an envelope into his back pocket. My curiosity and excitement grew as I tried to imagine what kind of adventure we were about to embark upon.

"Follow me," he whispered. We quickly tiptoed over to the side of the house, around the corner from the porch, and knelt down beside the small foundation window. He placed a finger over his chapped lips to indicate silence and I held my breath.

Then my father produced a small pocketknife and jammed it into the space between the window frame and the wooden casing. He wiggled the knife back and forth around the entire perimeter of the frame, prying it loose. Within a minute, he'd carefully removed the window and set it down next to the black opening.

The house sat atop a thick concrete slab, reinforced by steel rebar and elevated about three and a half feet above the ground. This left a small crawlspace under the first floor that could only be accessed from one of the two small windows on the foundation.

Slowly, my father leaned into the opening on his hands and knees. Then he picked up the lantern, held it up with an outstretched arm, and began to scan the entire area, sweeping back and forth from corner to corner. I crowded in under his other arm and poked my head into the opening beside him.

Though the footprint of the house covered no more than seven hundred square feet, the crawl-space seemed like an enormous cavern. A ribbon of sunlight poured in from the other window on the opposite side of the house; otherwise, no natural light reached into the silent, black space.

"What are you looking for, Dad?" I whispered.

"Rattlesnakes," he replied. "And tarantulas."

With that, I began to squirm and back away, but he grabbed me. "Now, don't worry about it; there aren't any down here. It's all clear. Trust me," he said with a chuckle, "if there were any snakes or spiders, I wouldn't go in either."

He then squeezed into the opening. "Come on," he whispered. I crawled in behind him, and then he turned, reached outside, and gently pulled the window into the casing to cover our tracks.

Though the mercury soared above 100 degrees on the porch thermometer, it was as comfortable as an early spring morning beneath the house. I dug my fingers into the cool, fine silt, never disturbed by wind and rarely reached by water during the decades that had passed since the structure was built. The air in this place was pleasant, and the sandy earth was as soft as a downy pillow—I could see why my father had brought me down here to this wonderful place, cramped as it was.

However, he had more to show. "Follow me over here," he rasped, craning his neck and turning his head sideways to look at me. He crawled toward the far corner of the house, his coveralls scraping the concrete overhead.

I scurried behind him in the dark, glancing every which way for silhouettes of rattlers, feeling more enthused and nervous than before.

I caught up to him. The lantern cast flashes of light across his shadowy face, and in the dust, pressed against the back wall, sat a small box. It was no surprise I'd not noticed it before—it was pure black, virtually absorbing the lantern light. A silver dial with numbers was in the middle of a small door on the front, with a handle beneath it and the word "Mosler" above it.

"What is it?" I asked, supposing it to be some peculiar birthday gift. "Is it for me?"

My father laughed quietly. "Well, sort of. This is my safe. I keep some of the most important things I have in here. Here, let me show you how you open it."

He took my hand in his and placed it on the dial.

"To open this safe, you have to remember three numbers. And it should be pretty easy because the numbers are your birthday: '8, 20, 26.' First, spin it three times to the right past zero. Then, stop on 8 for August." Together, we spun the dial as he gave instructions. I strained to see the numbers in the sparse, flickering glow.

"Then, turn it to the left and pass zero *twice*—then, stop on 20, the day you were born."

"Then go to 26, right?" I asked.

"Exactly. Let's turn it to the right, pass zero *once*,

and stop on 26. There," he said as he released my hand and cranked on the door handle. "It's open."

I eagerly anticipated seeing the inside of the mysterious box, but instead, my father slammed it shut and spun the dial around.

"Now you do it without my help."

•

It felt as though an eternity passed while I practiced, repeatedly unlocking the safe until I could do it effortlessly. Then he opened the door and moved the lantern closer to the wide-open mouth of the tiny coffer.

"I've been working at the dam for more than a year now," my father said in a hushed voice, reaching into the box. "And every time I come home, I add more money to my collection here under the house." An envelope stuffed with paper sat in his thick hands, and in the dark, crushing confines he looked like an unkempt troll hunched over a treasure.

"This is money that I will someday use to buy us all a house—you, me, your mom, and Grandpa too. But Grandpa doesn't want to move—well, neither do I—so that's why I'm hiding this money down here, where he won't know about it. So this is our secret. Got that?"

"Okay, Dad," I replied. What else you got in there?"

"Just some other things that I like. Pictures, mementos. Important stuff like that. No matter what happens, I feel like it will all be secure down here. It's stuff that I want you to have someday." Slowly,

37

he pulled another stack of currency out of his pants pocket and placed it in the strongbox. Then he closed the door.

"If anything ever happens and I can't get down here myself, you have to promise that you'll get it for me." I wasn't sure what he meant, but I agreed.

Above us, through the concrete, we heard faint footsteps.

"Mom and Grandpa are going to start wondering where we disappeared to. And this lantern's going to burn out any minute." He let out a sharp breath of air as he shifted his weight. "And my back is *killing* me. Let's be real quiet and real fast and crawl out of here, okay?"

8.

HOUSES AND TREES were disappearing from the streets like water evaporating from sand. During the winter, my grandfather and I would take long walks. How could we any other time of the year? It was a rare pastime. We often headed south away from town, in the direction of the old salt mines. As we walked by, we'd wave to the ranchers and farmers who lived on the southern outskirts of the village, rocking on their porches and sipping coffee after long days in the field.

And one late afternoon, in the early part of the winter of 1935, the three homes farthest from the downtown square were gone. They'd stood a week or two earlier. Now only slabs of gray concrete lay in the dust, like old headstones that had been tipped over. Even the aged cottonwoods that shaded the porches for decades had been felled, destroyed, cut down at the roots. Crops had begun to wither. Livestock that grazed day and night on scrubby desert brush had vanished. Now it was a barren, silent, arid wasteland.

It was no longer surprising to me when houses seemingly picked themselves up and walked away from St. Thomas. Still, losing three big farmhouses on some of the area's most valuable, verdant land was a bit of a shock. I took it all in for a moment, and then ran down the sandy and rutted road to catch my grandfather, who never broke stride.

"When?" I asked.

"Last week," Grandpa replied. Sometimes we didn't need many words to communicate. "Only took a few days. Sellar is in Overton. Pearson moved out to St. George."

"Guess they didn't want their cows and stuff to fall in the lake," I said.

"Don't start with that, boy."

A month later the dam would begin to impound water, and the lake would begin to make the long, slow crawl northward up the valley.

•

I wasn't really sure whom to believe: Dad or Grandpa? Would the waters drown us out like my father said? Or would the lake's shore stay far from town like my grandpa believed? I loved my dad, but I trusted my grandfather, because children believe to be true what they *want* to believe, and I wanted to believe that we'd never leave our home, that things would return to how they had been before. I didn't care what people said or that nearly everyone who lived in town had relocated or was planning to leave.

It was when the dead left town that I began to have doubts.

During early springtime in the desert, there are a few weeks of perfect, comfortable temperatures, when the winter chill has passed and the burning summer heat has not yet arrived. At every opportunity I would spend time outdoors, either in the old schoolyard, visiting my grandfather at his empty garage, or simply wandering the streets. And whenever I was given a small sum of money for candy, I would walk south to Gentry's Store.

On an early March afternoon, during my lunch break from lessons, I encountered Mr. and Mrs. Gentry on the street as I approached the store bearing their name. They had been dead since I was an infant.

Slowly bouncing down the road and bashing its way through potholes, a Ford stake truck carried a load of dirt-caked coffins, just removed from the cemetery at the southern end of the street. With every bump and thud, dried crumbles of mud rained down from the truck bed, and the stack of tightly packed wooden caskets shook and swayed.

As I stood on the sidewalk watching the eerie scene, I couldn't help but think how sacrilegious it seemed. All those people who'd been laid to rest in the town they had called home—a town that many of them had helped to settle—now being dragged out in the back of a truck to be unceremoniously dumped in some other place that hadn't meant a thing to them.

I thought about this while the pile of encased bodies rolled by. Suddenly, before I could even process and understand what I was seeing, the hairs on my neck stood on end and my heart jumped in my chest. The end piece of a casket had splintered and broken off while slamming into the stakes of the flatbed, and I could see inside. Wiry, gray hairs protruded from the top of a dry, gray skull, and with another few bumps, I thought it just might come rolling out and land plop in the road at my feet.

I turned and ran the rest of the block to Gentry's Store, where Ms. Gentry, daughter of the store's founders, was standing out in front, hands in the front pocket of her old blue apron, sadly watching the truck turn left onto Main Street and disappear.

"Well, there goes the last of them, including Mom and Dad," she said to me as I came to a stop. "You never got to know them too well, but they thought you were the cutest little baby they'd ever seen, Little Henry."

"Where . . . are they all . . . going?" I asked, gasping for breath.

"Overton. They're moving the whole cemetery to Overton. Everyone's going to have to get used to visiting their parents and grandparents in a whole new town." She sighed. "Well, let's go in. Do you want some chocolate?"

I had already completely lost my appetite for sweets. "No thanks, ma'am," I said as I turned and ran.

"Parents and grandparents," she'd said. *Hadn't Grandma Lord been buried in the St. Thomas*

Cemetery? I ran south out of town as fast as I could until I arrived at what had been the graveyard until that morning.

It looked like a field of giant anthills surrounded by a weathered split-rail fence. Piles of earth were scattered about, situated beside deep, empty holes. I felt my bowels swirling as my stomach dropped; my heart took refuge in my throat. I was still disturbed by the truckload of corpses I'd just seen, and now it looked like I was overlooking the site of a mass grave robbery.

I suppressed the creepy thoughts as best I could, stomping them back down into my subconscious, and forced myself to walk through the devastated grounds, being careful not to fall in and take the place of someone recently departed. Some of the headstones were still in place; most had been removed. A number of ancient wooden markers and rotting crosses, long since stripped of any identification by years of harsh weather, stood over empty graves.

I skirted six-foot-deep holes and prickly pears and wended my way through the cemetery until I came to a small granite monument that, oddly, was surrounded by undisturbed dirt. I read the epitaph:

Ann Lord
Wife and Mother
1877 – 1901

I backed away and nearly stumbled into an open grave, but I caught myself and turned and ran, slaloming between the empty pits. I sprinted home, eager to report my findings.

"Grandpa wouldn't let them move Grandma," my mom said matter-of-factly when I returned home for afternoon lessons. "Go into the bathroom and clean that sweat and dirt off your face. We need to get working on some arithmetic."

It really wasn't much of a surprise to either of us that my grandmother remained the only person buried in St. Thomas.

9.

WHEN FACED with hardship or tragedy, the perfunctory religious believer will do one of two things: he will delve deeper into his faith to search for comfort or a solution, or he will lose it entirely. My grandfather, already a long-time apostate of the Mormon Church, abandoned his faith when his wife died of influenza during my father's first year of life.

My mother, however, delved into prayer with fervor and purpose in the early summer of 1935. I'd rarely seen her pray before then, but I knew that when she resorted to asking favors of God, it meant she was troubled and desperate.

She began to pray nearly every night. I watched her one night—a hunchbacked silhouette in the dusk, illumed by an oil lantern, kneeling by the foot of her lonely bed. When she finished, I asked her why she prayed. She said she'd prayed when she was a girl for a husband, and it had brought my father to her, so maybe it would work again.

•

Since the previous summer when my father had revealed it to me, the secret spot beneath the house had become my refuge from the sun on hot days. And there is no shortage of scorching weather in a desert valley; eventually, it seemed as though I spent more time under the house than in it.

I never told my grandfather or my mother about the tight cellar space, and I would find it amusing when I'd hear them calling my name and stomping about, right above me or just outside the foundation window, oblivious to my whereabouts as I crouched in the sand reading books and comics and baseball card statistics by dim lantern light. It was especially amusing when I'd appear to them moments later, nonchalant, as if I'd been standing behind their backs all along.

During the weekend following the Independence Day holiday, a bit of activity stirred in the valley. There was a pretty pitiful fireworks display on Thursday, the Fourth, and on Friday and Saturday the scant few townsfolk tried to maintain a festive atmosphere. Bunting hung on the porches of homes now separated by vast vacant tracts, and a few firecrackers popped off every now and then. There were barbecues but no parades, save for a few drunks staggering down the avenues.

And unlike the previous year, my dad was not around. It had been nearly two months since he'd last made the trip home, and an air of melancholy hung about my family like a thick, stagnant fog. I wanted no part of it and retreated to the crawlspace to read.

It was July 6, 1935, but I had taken to the hills outside of Carson City in 1865 to mine for silver ore alongside Mark Twain. Then a woman's shrill cry made me drop my dog-eared copy of *Roughing It* in the dust and brought me back to the present. My pulse quickened, but I was suddenly afraid to move or make a sound. Gradually I began to shimmy across the ground, being careful to keep the lantern upright. From the western-facing window I could see a trail of dust following a car heading away from our home.

Then the shaft of daylight pouring through the window was eclipsed, and the dark shape of a human filled the opening, blocking out the sun. I crawled over and held up my lantern, and beyond the pane of glass my mother hunched in the dirt, peering in. Through the window my lamp cast light onto her pale face, twisted in agony. While I instantly realized that something horrible had happened, it also occurred to me that she knew exactly where I had been hiding and probably had known all along.

She said nothing, but tapped the glass with a fingertip. I pushed on the window and popped it out as she backed away. Then I crawled out.

"Your dad died," Mom announced before I could even stand up. "He had an accident and fell, and he's dead." With that last word, "*dead*," so painfully final, she broke down in tears and, still kneeling, threw her arms around me. I looked to the left and saw that my grandfather was standing beside us—eyes red and mouth hanging open, slack-jawed, stunned and awkward and lost. Then he too knelt with us and wrapped his arms around us both.

"I'm okay, I'm okay," my mom repeated. "Really, I'm okay." But the more she said it, the harder she wailed, and the tighter I squeezed her.

After his work as a high scaler had been completed, Dad took a job as a general laborer for Six Companies. As the official story goes, he fell from an incredible height, plunging from near the top of an intake tower on the Arizona side of the dam into the waters below. He likely died on impact; if not, he surely drowned, as his body was sucked into the roaring bowels of the spillway. I'm not sure why he fell. All that mattered then, and now, is that he was dead, *is* dead. Always will be dead. He fell into the lake and they found his body washed up on the river side of the dam. It swallowed him up and spit him out, waterlogged and limp. Bloated, pale, and chewed up.

We buried him in a closed casket ceremony in Overton just days later. Grandpa asked for a burial in St. Thomas, just north of the town center, but Mom wouldn't allow it.

I couldn't cry. I wanted to, terribly, but I couldn't.

•

Unfortunately, I also lost, for a time, the ability to sleep. I would pass entire nights in a half-wakened stupor that, later in life, I'd liken to a fall-down drunken haze. Frustrated with lying on my back unable to doze off, I'd sit upright, still, for countless hours at the foot of my bed, staring out my bedroom window, watching the moon trace an arc across the belly of the Milky Way. The heavens spread out for me in psychedelic patterns with shimmering auroras and shooting comets leaving temporary scars in my retinas, entire distant galaxies and worlds being born and dying before my eyes. But there was no sign of my father up there, or of anyone, for that matter, and I felt terribly alone and frightened in my damned desert valley floor town.

10.

WITHIN A WEEK of my father's death, I spent a night in the vacant schoolhouse just down the street from our home. I remember little of how I got there, as I was delirious with sleep deprivation, but I remember clearly how it was once I made it inside.

In a quasi-sleepwalking state, I somehow found my way through a broken window, coming to in one of the largest rooms, pitch dark and entirely empty. My quick breaths echoed off the bare walls and high ceiling. In my ears I could hear the loud drumming of my heart, and the floor creaked beneath my toes whenever I made a move. Every few seconds I was overcome with a horrible sensation of paranoia, as if I were being watched, but whenever I spun around or passed through an open doorway, I'd find no one. There were no ghosts, no vagrants. Only me. The aloneness was even more disturbing than being haunted or hunted.

Slowly, my eyes adjusted to the darkness, and I looked down at my hands, surprised to find that I wore my baseball glove. In its pocket sat a bright white baseball. It felt so natural to wear that I'd not even noticed I'd been carrying it the entire time. I pulled the ball out of the glove and held it in my right hand, feeling its weight in my fingertips. Then I fired it at an old blackboard still hanging on the wall; the ricochet made a noise like a thunderclap. I caught the ball as it rebounded off the floor and then hurled it again, as hard as I could. Over and over again I threw it full force until the writing surface began to spider-web and splinter. Finally it shattered, and shards fell to the floor in a pile.

Nothing had felt right for a while—but destruction felt right. If I couldn't release my grief by crying or find momentary peace in slumber, then I would purge by unleashing my wrath.

I stomped through the big old building and threw the ball at the chalkboards and walls. I smashed a pencil sharpener that protruded from a doorframe and knocked it to the floor. A small Nevada flag sat on a windowsill, and I easily shredded the rotten, sun-bleached material in my fists. While I pulled the fabric to ribbons, a sudden thought came to me: *This should be where I go to school. I should sit at a desk here in these rooms with other kids, and I should play tag and hide-and-seek and baseball with them in the yard. My mom would sit at the front of the room, and at the end of the day we'd walk home together, and then we'd go visit Dad and Grandpa at the garage—*

God, how could I have tortured myself like this? My thoughts had run away from me, and the idea of how things *should* be was overwhelming. I let out an anguished roar that broke the silence in the black room and scared me half to death, as I barely recognized it as a noise that could have come from my own throat. But it didn't stop my rampage. I ascended the stairs to the second floor and found trash, old books with broken spines, and busted desks and chairs and bookcases, and in a rage I caused as much destruction as possible until at last, exhausted, I launched the baseball through a pane of glass and climbed an old wooden ladder to the cupola, where I fell into a deep dreamless sleep among clumps of dust and dried bat dung.

When I awoke I realized it was late morning, as the sun had already risen quite high in the sky, and my skin was glazed with sweat. Though rested for the first time since before my father's death, I felt as if I could have continued to sleep for another several hours. But two loud voices from far below in the street had interrupted my slumber, and they were crying my name: "*Henry! Where are you?*"

Brushing myself off, I peeped over the edge of the open cupola.

"I'm up here," I said as my mother and grandpa passed directly beneath me. They both stopped dead in their tracks, nearly toppling over with shock and confusion. At last they located me, looking up with expressions of both relief and anger. Mostly relief.

"Henry! What the heck are you doing up there?" asked my grandfather.

"Nothing," I replied. "What are you doing down there?"

11.

OVER THE NEXT several years, my grandfather showed aplomb whenever neighbors, friends, and government officials questioned his decision to stay, and his confidence that the lake would never reach the town seemed to grow enormously. Looking south, you could see the waters of Lake Mead creeping toward us, beautiful and ominous. Yet every time the lake seemed as though it were making a final advance, it would abruptly retreat several hundred feet back down the valley.

I sometimes walked to the water, alone. I would catch myself almost admiring its beauty—a lake in the desert, an out-of-place alien being. But then I'd remember the pain it had caused my family, and an image of my father's body at the bottom of this artificial sea would force itself into my mind even though

I knew he was buried in a lonesome private plot in Overton.

Grandpa never came to the water with me. To him, the lake could not have been more repellant and odious if it lapped at the shore with waves of ammonia and sulfur. And my mother rarely left the house anymore. She'd become so withdrawn that I'd been forced to attend school in Overton; she no longer had the gumption or desire to continue homeschooling.

In the winter of 1936, halfway through my fourth-grade studies, I started making the trip to Overton each day. It was more than eight miles from our home to the schoolhouse, but because of the lack of business at the garage, save for pity appointments from old acquaintances, Grandpa had plenty of time to drive me in the old pickup. At home, around my mom, he generally remained quiet, but during the drives to and from school he would let down his guard and talk my ear off, ranting, mostly, about all the ills of the world and the wrongdoings of young folk, the evils of government and power and the corrupting influences of money and the damage caused by technology and progress—a fractured and confused verbal manifesto of self-righteousness rooted in paranoia, stubbornness, and fear of change; the same monotonous, conventional angst that collects like cobwebs in the minds of the elderly in all generations. Offended fools with wounded morals.

Add to his choler the death of a son, a failing business, and a destroyed community—I too shared and shouldered a great deal of his despair. But while everyone else accepted fate, my grandfather was like a man seated at the base of a rumbling volcano, preferring to be engulfed by lava and flames than to acquiesce to the inevitable and vacate—and never really believing that he would lose all that he'd built and loved, even if he'd already lost most of it.

So I let him talk. I think he would have even if I hadn't been sitting there. The drives were good for him, as they gave him a reason to get out of St. Thomas and see the nearby community. Perhaps, I thought, he would connect with old neighbors and see that Overton was much the same as what St. Thomas had once been. Wishful thinking on my part, I suppose.

There were days when my grandfather wasn't waiting for me after school, and I'd walk most or all of the way home, sometimes covering nearly the entire distance. I looped my thumbs around the straps of my heavy pack to loosen the pinch, and all the while it thumped against my rear in time with my meandering steps. I kicked rust-red stones, watched sparrows and tarantulas scatter in my presence, and pondered my world. The road out of Overton toward St. Thomas was desolate, and from the lonesome plateau it traversed I could look down on my small hometown dissolving into the surrounding desert. Tamarisk choked the now vacant farmlands, and brush sprang up in the dead and dry parcels that were once shady, green homesteads. And in the distance, glassy and scattering the late afternoon sunlight like sparkling prism crystals, the tip of Lake Mead loomed, inching up the Muddy River into the Moapa Valley.

•

At first, it was difficult to adapt to school. I had never in my life attended a public schoolhouse and had rarely even encountered children of my own age, let alone studied alongside and played with them.

"Hey! Where'd *you* come from?" a short kid in a jacket and overalls said during my first week of school. We were outside on the playground after lunch, bundled up because it was January. I stood near a swing set waiting for a turn and suddenly found myself in the center of a semicircle of blond-haired boys.

I made eye contact with the boy who spoke and recognized right away that he intended to fight me. Well, what could I do? There was nowhere to go, and I wasn't about to go run to a teacher and hide behind a dress.

"I live in St. Thomas," I replied evenly. "With my mom and my grandpa. I'm new here."

"Yeah? What kind of screwballs still live down in that old place?"

"We're not screwballs. I've always lived there, for my whole life."

He and his friends forced a laugh. "Well, what do you do down there all day?"

I could see there were going to be no correct answers to any of his questions, and a girl had just jumped off a swing, so I answered, "Not much. I'm going to get on a swing now, okay?"

"My dad says nobody got any reason to be down there in that ghost town," he replied, inching forward.

What I said next was solely the result of spending so much time alone; of having no social training and no experience interacting with other children; of reading constantly and learning from a mother whose love of the English language was surpassed perhaps only by her love for her son and her now-deceased husband. It just slipped out of my mouth, and I wished I could take it back the moment I said it.

"Nobody *has* any reason . . . to be down . . . there," I corrected him, my words trailing off into a whisper.

For a brief moment the boy stood with his mouth agape, stunned. Then, without saying a word, he stepped forward and shoved me, slamming the palms of his hands into my collarbone. I stumbled backward and fell to the ground, landing on my elbows in the gravel, and his knees fell onto my chest. The wind burst from my lungs like a popped balloon. Ringed by newly made enemies shouting and cheering him on, I lay limp, taking the beating while other children in the schoolyard flocked around to watch.

The kid was smaller than me and not very strong, and I was pretty certain I could have whipped him if I'd wanted to. But after what I'd said, I figured I deserved it. Besides, it didn't hurt too much. His thumbs were wrapped inside his fingers, and instead of punching straight, he swatted at me like he was shooing flies. With my heaviest jacket providing extra padding, I could barely feel a thing. Still, he was able to split my lower lip and give me a bloody nose before a teacher hauled him off and broke up the crowd. Of course, in the dry desert, it doesn't take too much trauma for a nose to start bleeding or a dry lip to split.

I brushed myself off and washed my face in the boys' room sink, satisfied that I'd paid my penance. I made up my mind, however, that I'd fight back the next time he started anything with me. And he *did* start something with me the very next week. Zachary Young, that was his name. With a single knockdown punch to the jaw, I ended that fight before it even had a chance to get started—the teacher never even saw it happen. Once we started playing baseball a few weeks later and the boys saw my strong arm and my slick glove, I didn't have any further problems with fights or making friends. Zach even picked me first to be on his team.

But I felt deeply wounded—mentally, if not physically—on the day of the fight. I shuffled around the schoolyard, alone, hanging my head and kicking up dust while waiting for the truck to roll up. I already knew what would happen: my grandfather would make me swear vicious and immediate retribution the moment he saw me, while my mother would fret and coddle me. Nobody showed up though, and I walked for hours, almost the entire stretch home, before my grandfather's pickup truck materialized around a bend, blinding me in the twilight with its headlights. I hopped into the cab.

He was predictably apoplectic, but I promised to take care of business myself—and eventually, I did. However, my mother's reaction was far different than I'd imagined.

It was dark when we arrived home, and I found her upstairs in my bedroom placing clean laundry in my dresser drawer. She wore a thin white dress that hung down to her feet, the ivory fabric matching the pallid skin of her face and arms. Bathed in the cool glow of the oil lantern's flame, she looked less like my mother than like the ghost of my mother.

"Hi, Mom," I said.

"Hello, dear," she said, gliding over to kneel down to kiss me. But she stopped short and turned to grab the lantern. She held it up to inspect my wounds, blinding me.

"What happened?" she asked flatly, sounding hardly concerned. "Looks like you had some sort of accident."

"Not really," I replied. "I got in a little fight. It's no big deal. I'm okay."

"You shouldn't be fighting."

"I didn't," I confessed, feeling slightly embarrassed. "I kind of just sat there."

"Maybe go wash up."

"I already did, Mom."

"Your father wouldn't like you fighting. There's just no reason for it." She sighed deeply and turned away, looking out the window into black nothingness. "I worry about you. He worried about you. I don't want you to get hurt or have an accident."

"What do you mean?" I asked, feeling exasperated. "I didn't start any fight and I didn't have any accident."

Then she paused and studied the shirt she was folding, stroking it, as if lost in thought. Then she put it down and opened the gold locket that she kept on a chain around her neck to study a small photo of my father.

"I know, honey," she said at last. "You didn't have an accident today. But they can happen at any time. They're *always* waiting to happen." She stopped again and squeezed the garment in her fists. "But they're not always a bad thing. Did you know it was because of an accident that your father and I met?"

Until then, I'd never even considered that there had been a time that my parents didn't know each other. The idea of their meeting as strangers struck me as odd, almost unpleasant. But she continued before I could respond.

"It was. It was just an accident. It was in December of 1925, and my dad was taking me out for a drive. He'd just gotten a beautiful Model T shipped down from Salt Lake that very day. It was something he'd been saving up to buy for a long time. He always promised the family that someday we'd take trips to Salt Lake and Los Angeles in style." She laughed hoarsely. "That was important to your grandfather: that we'd go *in style*. I would have been happy taking the railroad, but we never went anywhere on a train.

"So we finally got a car. It was beautiful, red on the outside with gold trim, and it had soft, black, velvety seats and a black top to give us shade. We had been waiting for it for weeks, and when it arrived it was like Christmas had come early. My sister and I jumped into the back seat while Mom—I mean, your grandma—sat up front with Grandpa. We rode all over town, all through the valley, showing off. We drove to the post office and the store, and we went by the hotel where all the people from California stayed with their fancy cars—and none were as beautiful as ours.

"Then Daddy got the idea that we should drive a little way out toward Utah. He'd only ever driven a couple times before and had no idea of just how far it was . . . but we were all so excited, so we went for it. We left town and crossed the bridge over the river. I felt like I was having the adventure of my life! And then all of a sudden there was a *bang*, like we were being shot at. And the car swerved and we went right off the road and came to a stop in a big patch of prickly pear."

She sat down at the foot of my bed next to a small pile of neatly folded laundry, crossed her legs at the knees, and set her hands in her lap, fingers intertwined. She stared in my direction, though I knew she was not looking at me, nor at anything in the room we occupied.

"Two tires were blown out. Can you believe that? Two! And on our very first drive! We walked all the way back to town and straight into Grandpa Henry's auto shop, and that was the first time I met your father. Of course, I'd seen him around town before, but it was the first time we were introduced properly. We were married within a year, and I moved into this house and started teaching just after the wedding."

"That's a nice story, Mom," I interjected, hoping, but not really believing, the tale to be complete. I trembled slightly, knowing in my gut that her rambling tale was not heading toward a happy conclusion. And after the day's events in the schoolyard, followed by the long walk through the desert in the dusk, I wasn't quite sure how much more I could endure.

She went on. "You see? Accidents. It was an accident that brought your father and me together, and it was an accident that took him from us. Just like it was an accident that took my parents and sister, the fire that burned them up while they were sleeping. Little accidents: flat tires, spilled oil lanterns. Accidents give, and accidents can take it all away."

I'd never known my maternal grandparents and aunt, and until then I'd never known how they had died. But now the truth of things fell on me like a pile of bricks, and I suddenly understood the burden of loss my mother shouldered every day. In barely a decade's time she had endured the tragic losses of her parents, sibling, and husband, as well as her job. By the age of 30 the foundation of her life had crumbled and burned, and it lay at her feet like a pile of ashes, never to be put back together.

She began to cry. At that moment I wanted nothing more than to move far, far away from St. Thomas. My grandfather's stubbornness had kept us rooted in quicksand, and it was rapidly swallowing my mother. Why wouldn't he just let us leave and start over?

"I don't want to leave town," said my mother. I felt goose bumps pop up all over my body as I became, for a moment, convinced that she could read my thoughts. "Grandpa doesn't want to leave either. And you want to stay, right?"

"It's okay," I said softly. "I—I don't mind if we move. I'd be happy, and you'd be happy. Wouldn't you?"

"No, I wouldn't," she snapped, rubbing the tears from her face with her crumpled shirtsleeves. "My whole life has been spent *here*. If we leave, we'll give up everything. It will be just like we never even *existed*. What part of our past are we leaving for the future?"

It was a rhetorical question; I could offer no answer. She stood up and walked out briskly, carrying the lantern, leaving me in the dark.

12.

SEVERAL MONTHS LATER, in the middle of spring, my grandfather bought a boat. It wasn't much—certainly nothing like the speedboats and sloops that would come to populate the surface of Lake Mead. But when he unexpectedly showed up one Sunday afternoon with a little aluminum dinghy in the bed of the pickup, I bolted out the front door feeling as excited as if he'd towed home the *Queen Mary*.

"Grandpa, you bought a boat?" I shouted as I leaped from the porch and landed barefoot in the sandy driveway. "You bought a *boat!*"

"Well, that's what it looks like," he said reservedly, one hand in his pocket, the other patting the dull metallic hull. He didn't sound too keyed up, but we shared a glance and his eyes flickered with a light that I could scarcely remember seeing before.

I wrapped my hands around the top of the tailgate of the truck, ignoring the sensation of searing hot metal in my palms, and pulled myself up onto the rear bumper to get a better look at our new toy. Attached to the rear of the boat was a bizarre little machine—a silvery contraption, sort of like the old ice cream mixer at Hannig's—with what looked like cranks and pipes and blades sticking out of it. "Evinrude" was emblazoned across it, which explained nothing of its purpose to me.

"What's that there on the back of it?" I asked.

"That's an outboard motor. It cost me a pretty penny, but I can't expect you to row me around all the time," he said with a chortle and a wry grin.

In my excitement, I failed to filter my thoughts and blurted out, "We're going to take it out on the lake?"

"Damn it, *no!*" he barked, his face knotting up into a sour grimace. "I won't *look* at that son of a bitch lake, let alone take a boat out on it!" But he composed himself quickly and said in a soft voice, "No, we're going to take this up the Muddy and the Virgin Rivers. And I got something else for us too." He reached through the open window of the truck and pulled out a couple straw hats and two brand-new fishing rods. I hopped off the bumper of the truck and reached for the cork handle of the rod as he passed it over to me. "I figure you ought to know how to fish, so I'm gonna teach you. To get to the *good* spots, we're gonna have to go upstream from here, so that engine will give us a hand to get there. We'll be pulling trout and chub out of that water before you know it, and we got a couple months of fishing ahead of us before the water drops in the summer."

Those were the best plans I'd ever heard. I threw my arms around his waist and hugged him tight, my eyes clenched and my cheek pressed against his chest. He hugged me back, one hand on my upper back and the other cupped at the nape of my neck, the same way my father used to hold me. For a brief second I almost thought it really *was* my dad I was embracing. When I let go I looked up at my grandfather and saw him smiling tenderly, as if there were a part of my father he had kept tucked away within him that was just now beginning to surface, chiseling at the ornery barricade he'd spent a lifetime erecting and cowering behind. Grandpa brought up my dad; raised him on his own. But when I reflect on that moment—as well as on moments in my own life when I realize I owe much to my own children for the person I have become—sometimes, I think, sons raise their fathers too.

•

The day was still young, and though the sun hung in a bright blue and cloudless sky, the springtime air was pleasantly crisp. Grandpa had picked up some bait from Gentry's (a few chunks of day-old bread and a canteen of maggots), and we drove way out past where the old Syphus farm used to be and parked at the base of a stony bluff about thirty feet from the bank of the Muddy.

He was getting older but seemed none the worse for wear, physically—my grandfather threw down the tailgate with a *boom* and dragged the boat from the truck bed, slowly lowering it to the sandy duff. Then he placed a couple oars and a small gas can in the dinghy, as well as our fishing gear, and circled around to the bow.

"Okay, Henry, you need to help me carry the boat over to the water," he explained. "Come over here and grab this rope; it's tied to the bow. That's what you call the front of a boat. I don't need you to lift it high up—just enough so that the bottom isn't scraping the ground too badly. I'll pick it up at the stern where the engine is and carry most of the weight. All right?"

"I can do that," I assured him.

With caution, we scuffled over to the water's edge and placed the rowboat by the lazily drifting river. I swished my hands around in the water and marveled at how even in the desert the river could feel so cold. Grandpa filled the small motor with gasoline, and within minutes we shoved off and puttered along upstream.

The pleasant thrum of the motor vibrated my body to the core, and the faint scent of burning gasoline mixed with the grassy smell of the rarefied cattails and sedge cropping up along the riverbanks. Damselflies and dragonflies, metallic blue and green-gold, zipped around and hovered like helicopters just inches from my nose. The oceanic desert spread out endlessly on both sides of the water, and in its midst I had found paradise. Judging by the contented look on my grandpa's face as he calmly manned the motor, he had too.

After a while we pulled into a small, shadowy cove where the river bellied out toward a crumbling ten-foot-high wall of red rock and dried mud. Peering over the edge of the boat, I could see schools of small fish twitching and jolting through the clear water in unison, instinctively reacting to my every overhead motion. The small anchor was lowered into the river, and my grandfather, satisfied that we had found our ideal spot, leaned down and picked up his pole.

For the next twenty minutes or so I sat through a crash course in fishing, learning how to tie the hook, weight, and bobber to the line, how to thread grubs onto the hook (or bread scraps, which I preferred), and the proper techniques of casting the line and reeling it in. Then I sat through a detailed explanation of how to remove a hook from the lip of the fish. "Which," my grandpa said, "is something that will be easier to show you once you catch one. And this looks like a great spot, so I think we'll have no problem hooking a whole bunch of fish."

"But where do I *put* the fish once I get it off the hook, Grandpa?" I asked. "Shouldn't we have a bucket or something so we can take them home for dinner?"

"Good question," he said as he threaded a squirming maggot onto my hook. I found it odd that he should do it for me just as he'd finished teaching me how to do it myself. "Today we're throwing 'em back. It's a practice day for you, just to get the hang of it.

Maybe we can come back out tomorrow and catch some dinner. What do you say?"

"Okay!" I agreed as he handed the pole over to me. I waited for him to thread bait onto his own hook, and then we cast our lines together, his flying more than twice as far as mine and nearly landing in a salt-cedar thicket on the shore.

"Nice, nice job there," he said proudly. "Give it a little tug like I showed you. Let those little fishies know that you've got some dinner for 'em." I tugged gently. Nothing happened. I kept tugging; the squirming bait danced in the water.

We were both people of few words, and fishing is a sport that demands hushed voices and a slight degree of concentration. For us it was shared, quiet joy.

Two mallard ducks, a male and a female, flew downstream and landed in the cove like jets on a runway, side by side. "Shoo!" whispered Grandpa, waving a hand toward the feathered intruders. But they refused to leave our side and circled about our boat, curious and hungry.

Nearly fifteen minutes passed. My grandfather let out a sigh. "I'm a bit surprised we haven't gotten any nibbles yet," he said. "Henry, why don't you reel your line in, and let's see if your bait didn't fall off or get snatched."

I followed his direction and began to bring in my line, my right hand whizzing in a circle as I cranked the reel handle. Suddenly—I felt a jolt! *Is the line snagged?* I thought. No! The end of the rod began to vibrate and bend, curving down toward the river's surface, and the line was pulled as taut as a kite string.

"Grandpa, Grandpa!" I shouted, bouncing up in my seat. "I've got something here!"

His face lit up like a Christmas tree. "Yep, you surely do!" he exclaimed. "Okay, be gentle now and reel her in carefully. Don't go too fast, but don't let the line go slack! Let 'er fight you a bit. Good job! Reel it back a little bit more . . ."

He set his own fishing pole down and shimmied across the boat on his knees, scuffing the frayed denim of his pants. I felt his hands on my shoulders as he continued to guide me. I thought maybe he'd take the rod from me, but he let me have the fight all to myself.

"Nice job, Henry . . . almost got it . . . there we go!"

Thrashing and splashing, a massive trout exploded out of the water at the end of my line. Simultaneously, the pair of ducks burst out of the water and flew like missiles toward the safety of the bushes on the shore, no longer interested in the goings-on in and around our tiny craft.

I hefted the fish out of the water. It was a gorgeous bull trout, nearly as long as my arm and glistening in the sun as it thrashed about, tossing beads of river water into my face. Pale gold spots flecked its olive green back, and its soft belly was a creamy orange-pink hue, the color of the sky as the sun falls behind the desert hills and sets fire to the clouds.

"Ha ha, yeah!" I laughed, triumphantly.

"What a beaut, Henry!" shouted my grandfather

as he grabbed the middle of the rod to stabilize it. And then, just as abruptly as he'd sprung up when I'd hooked the fish, he grimaced as his eyes filled with concern.

I looked back at the trout, gasping and flailing. Now, it occurred to me that the line seemed to disappear into its wide-open mouth.

"Uh, Grandpa?" I ventured. "I don't see the hook. Isn't the hook supposed to be in the fish's lip?"

"Mmm," he grunted. As he assessed the situation, his lips pressed together tightly, forming a horizontal line across his tan, wrinkly face. "It swallowed the hook, damn it."

"Well, let's pull it out."

He glanced at me without replying, contemplating his next words.

"Can't you pull it out?"

"No," he answered. "If a fish swallows a hook, that means it's in his belly, or close to it. If you pull it out you'll shred his guts to ribbons—also, you'd probably pull out some of its organs. You don't want to make it suffer."

"So what do we do?" I asked, still grasping at the hope that he'd have a good solution.

He pinched the line just above where it vanished into the trout. "Let out a little bit of line," he ordered. "I need a bit of slack." I released a bit of line, and it draped down into the water, floating on the surface.

Then, in one swift motion, he wrapped his free hand around the tail of the fish.

CRACK!

Before I knew what was happening, he swung the fish down and slammed the back of its skull into the narrow edge of the boat. It squirted out of his hands like a greased melon and landed with a slimy *splat* on the floor of the boat. It shivered for a moment, its tailfin curling, and then it relaxed and lay limp. I sat, frozen, looking at one silver eye, loose in its socket, gazing through me and into the sun, seeing nothing. Streams of blood as red as mine slowly oozed out its mouth, eyeholes, and gills.

"Mmm," grumbled Grandpa again. "What a shame that had to happen on your very first fish. Doesn't happen too terribly often." He looked up at me and saw that I was trembling and just about to start crying.

"But it happens," he said, changing his tune and getting tougher with me. "It's not too pleasant, but we're going to be catching and eating them anyway, Henry, so don't worry about it. This guy didn't suffer, and later, maybe we can eat him for dinner."

But we'd intended to throw back everything we caught, so we had no bucket. Grandpa tried to salvage the fish by pouring a bit of water into the bottom of the boat to keep it somewhat fresh, but by the time we got back to the bank where the truck was parked, the trout was starting to smell, floating in a warm soup of water and its own blood. We dropped it in the sand beside a patch of brittlebush with yellow flowers in full bloom.

"Something will come by and eat this. And it'll be grateful for the meal."

13.

I DIDN'T FISH too much after that. I thought Grandpa would be disappointed, but he didn't seem to be bothered. I think he was just happy to have company out on the water. We went out together as often as we could. Other than on the baseball diamond, I felt more at home on the river than anywhere else, reading books and watching the birds flit by. And nowhere else had I found as much peace.

But as the days and months rolled by, Lake Mead continued to grow with abandon, expanding up the rivers, up the Moapa Valley, reaching ominously toward our village. Just south of town, where the Muddy once vanished beyond Gold Butte, way down toward the old Bonnelli Ferry landing on the Colorado, it was water, water everywhere. Even some of the former farmland, teeming with crops and cattle only a few short years prior, was now partially flooded, and the desert flora that had just taken root in place of the rows of irrigated wheat was now being drowned.

And the holdouts? Only the most stubborn, absolutely foolhardy souls remained. Nobody was rushing to our sides to raise a dike or divert the waters; no end was in sight for the relentless advance of the desert sea, voraciously devouring all the terrain in its path.

Businesses had fled. We were left with a single store, rarely open, and a post office to serve the remaining dozen or so denizens. Some held their breath, hoping that perhaps the nearby Valley of Fire to the west, just christened as a state park in '35, would renew interest in our town. But nobody came.

•

It was late spring in 1938 when the water finally entered St. Thomas. Southeast of our house, the Pearson, Armfield, and Sellar homesteads sank by inches beneath the surface of the lake. Worse, out on the lonely southwest corner of town, the old graveyard (with its solitary occupant) was soaked through. The bleached split-rail fence fell to pieces and floated away, and six feet below the brand new lakebed, freshwater crept into the long-buried casket of my grandmother.

Soon after, the water approached Route 91. Across the street, the old schoolyard where I'd spent my youth throwing baseballs against the façade of the school was spongy and wet. Soon the lake would be in our front yard.

The message finally got through to Grandpa: the time to leave before all was lost was fast approaching. Late one June evening, when I was supposed to be sleeping, I could hear my grandfather settle into his rocker in the living room beside the old barrister bookcase, upon which sat one of the brightly burning oil lanterns for reading. I expected to hear nothing but the intermittent whisper of turning pages as I drifted to sleep. Instead, I heard the words I'd thought I'd never hear.

"I took a drive around Overton today after I dropped off Henry at school," my grandfather said matter-of-factly. "I'm thinking I found a few spots that might work for us up there." He was careful to not use the words "new home," or "house," as if the words spoken in the confines of the home he'd clung to for so long would be sacrilege.

"Oh?" replied my mother, as though it were a trivial piece of information. "Well, whatever you think is best."

"I wouldn't mind showing them to you and Henry this weekend. This week I should be able to get Whitmore and the Bunkers to help me relocate the shop up to higher ground. We can buy one of the properties downtown near the school and we can set it up there, just the same as it is here. Maybe you can even start teaching again."

The words were remarkably sanguine, I thought, coming from a man who'd shunned every opportunity to move and for years had laughed in the face of anyone who suggested that the lake would actually breach the town's border.

My mother didn't offer any reply—at least, none that I could hear. "I can make a meeting at the bank next week," offered my grandfather, "and we can figure out a mortgage payment. I might even be able to pay off the whole thing."

"I could put up some money too," my mother said. "I can help out."

"What money do *you* have?" Grandpa scoffed. But my mom, once clever and quick to reply, now a listless shell of her pre-widowed self, withheld an answer. Or maybe I didn't hear her response, or perhaps I fell asleep. Regardless, to my ears, the conversation was over.

14.

THE NEXT DAY was the last day of school for the year, and at the end of lessons I was surprised to find my grandfather waiting for me outside, sitting in his idling truck. I expected that he was going to take me to look at houses around town, or perhaps show me where he was setting up a new shop. But instead we headed straight back to St. Thomas. Alas, as I wasn't supposed to have heard any of the previous night's conversation, I couldn't directly express my confusion.

"What's going on, Grandpa?" I asked. "Why are you here so early today?"

"I've been waiting all day to get out on the river, boy," he said. "But I didn't want to take off without you."

"Really?" I said with astonishment, knowing how much work had to be done. "We're going fishing?"

"Yeah. Why not?" he replied. "It's perfect out. We're not going to get many more days like this."

I knew, for my sake, he was referring to the weather. But the implication was even clearer: we were down to the end of our days in St. Thomas. It was a last hurrah of sorts. Sure, the rivers weren't going anyplace. But it was likely to be the last time we'd ever pass by the shady old cottonwood at the edge of our driveway, turn the corner past the long-abandoned Hannig's and the longer-abandoned blacksmith shop, and rumble out across the crusty salt flat northeast of town to our docking spot at the bend in the river.

●

We parked the truck and jumped out. Grandpa plucked his fishing rod from behind the seat in the truck's cab—mine hadn't been touched in some time—and I grabbed a couple hardcover books from my pack. Then he slid the boat out of the truck bed and dropped his pole, bait canteen, and tackle box in. By now, I knew the routine: I placed our water canteens and my books in the bow, picked up the slackened rope, and marched down to the water to shove off.

It was not quite three o'clock in the afternoon, but being early summer, we still had hours and hours of daylight ahead. The mercury must have been inching its way up the thermometer though, as often happens in late afternoon in the desert. It's always hottest just before dusk, and we were feeling it.

"Getting pretty warm out," I shouted over the blare of the engine as I doffed my hat and wiped sweat from my brow.

"Hell is an icebox by comparison," my grandfather quipped.

Often, we stopped to drop anchor at the cove where we'd fished on our first expedition, about two miles up from our launch point. But on this day we breezed right by. "I'm heading up the river a little farther," said Grandpa. "I heard there's a pool of chub another few miles up where they're snapping like crazy, and I could go for a little action today. Think I might do a little fly fishing."

"Sounds good to me. As long as there's some shade."

And shade it had plenty of—the inlet we pulled into was canopied by a group of large desert-willow trees drooping their tangled branches out over the softly swirling waters. We came to a stop in the center of their shadows and lowered the anchor. The air felt cool and comfortable, and I took a swig from my canteen with one hand while digging out a book with the other.

My grandpa broke open his tackle box and began to thread a lure onto the line. I could tell by the way he kept opening his mouth and letting out a sigh that he wanted to speak, but couldn't find the words. Finally, as he cast his first line, he let it out.

"Well . . . I emptied out the shop today," he admitted sadly.

"Really? Where did you take all of your equipment?" I asked, feigning astonishment.

"It took me and Whitmore most of the day and about ten truckloads each to get it up to his new property in Overton. He's got most of his furniture and belongings moved already. I helped him out the last couple days. He should be completely moved in by tomorrow." He cleared his throat. "Heck, he might even be there tonight. Guetzill's been moving; Perkins too. Bunkers moved all their stuff last week."

"Looks like we're the last ones to stick it out in St. Thomas," I said.

"Yep," Grandpa said and let out a long sigh. "We did all we could. Waited it out as best we could. I didn't think it would come to this though, Henry. I really didn't."

"I think we'll be happy in a new place. You, me, and Mom. It will be just like it is now, except we won't have to worry about a lake sneaking up and drowning us out. The garage will do better too, don't you think?"

"I think so. I think we're going to be just fine. I was considering this weekend I'd take you and your mom up into town to look at some property, but the way the water is moving in these days, we'd better start looking tomorrow."

"Yep," I said, unintentionally mimicking him. With all the time we spent together, it's no wonder that I'd begun to affect some of his mannerisms.

But it had just occurred to me: I needed to get under the house and empty out my dad's safe. I couldn't believe it hadn't come to mind earlier that I needed to rescue my father's most precious belongings—as well as the money he'd ultimately traded his life to earn. I hadn't been under the house but once or twice in the three years since he'd died, as it only made me feel wretchedly, painfully sad. It was our secret spot together, and it was where I was hiding when I learned of his death.

8, 20, 26. My birthday. I still remembered the combination. I would get up early in the morning, well before sunrise and before anyone else awoke, and quickly empty the contents of the safe into my backpack. No one would ever know. It would remain a secret between Dad and me.

It was settled. I had a mission. For the time being, however, I would lean back in the boat in the shade, sipping water and reading Thoreau. My mom had given me a copy of *Walden* to read "when I had some time"—and there was no better time than now, on the river, after school had let out for the year.

But eventually the book dropped to my chest. I pulled my hat down low, listened to the swish of the breeze in the leaves of the trees, and fell into a deep slumber.

15.

MY EYES POPPED open wide, and a chill ran down my spine. Had I dreamed that deep, booming roll of thunder?

No. A second clap echoing the first confirmed that it was real.

The wide brim of my hat and the big book fanned out across my torso had kept most of my upper body dry, but I quickly realized that my jeans were cold, wet, and sticking to my legs. I strained to sit up, my body stiff and sore, and tried to determine where I was. Then it came to me: we were in the boat, on the river, miles from home.

A light mist had glazed the boat and everything in it, but the thunderheads were growling, promising an imminent, fierce downpour, the kind that gives desert dwellers nightmares of flash floods and mudslides. A tenebrous shade of purple that deepened to navy in the east colored the evening sky, and I estimated that there was less than an hour to complete and total darkness. I must have slept for three, four hours. Maybe more.

Slowly, I crawled up onto my seat. Then I looked across the boat at Grandpa. He lay motionless, sprawled out with his hat over his face, neck crooked in a painful-looking position as his head slumped against the engine. His arms flailed out and his legs rested up on the bench seat. The fishing rod crossed over his chest like a sash, and water had begun to pool around his body, soaking his flannel shirt and jeans.

For the second time in barely two minutes, goose-flesh crawled up my back. How could he be sleeping through this? Maybe my eyes were playing tricks on me in the twilight, but I could not make out the rise and fall of his chest. I held my own breath, shaking, fearing the worst.

"G-grandpa?" I said, barely audible over the clatter of rain.

"What? *What?* I'm awake!" he shouted, jolting up and nearly capsizing the boat as he threw his weight around. "Holy *hell*, what is going on? I'm sopping! Henry, why were you letting me sleep through this?" He scrambled back into his seat, the heels of his boots slipping on the wet aluminum.

"I was sleeping too!" I yelled back, angry that I was being blamed for our situation, but also relieved that he wasn't dead. "I just woke up a second ago, and then I woke *you* up!"

But he wasn't listening. Grandpa yanked on the engine cord once, twice, three times, and it finally started up, eliciting a huge sigh of relief from the both of us. I pulled up the anchor from the dark waters and we spun around, aiming downstream toward home.

Just then, far up in the troposphere but directly overhead, a forked bolt of lightning arced sidelong across the sky, illuminating the river and mountains in white light. I turned to look back at my grandfather, and the taut expression of fear on his face did little to console me.

"I can think of a few places I'd rather be right now," I shouted.

"You and me both, boy."

"How far to the truck?" I asked, but a massive roar of thunder swallowed the words as they came forth from my mouth.

"What did you say?" yelled Grandpa.

"*How far is it to the truck?*"

"*Too* far! About five, six miles, I'd say! Take us forty-five minutes to an hour at least, unless we have to refuel, in which case it might take us *longer!*"

I turned around to look out over the river, dimpled with fat raindrops that seemed to pop back up out of the water as soon as they touched down. Ceaseless flashes of lightning, the kind you think only exist in horror films, crackled in the sky, and cold, wet terror seized my trembling body.

•

I've had whole years of my life go by that felt quicker than the time it took us to travel down that section of the Muddy. Even though the cracks of lightning and rolls of thunder demanded that we go faster, we trawled at a turtle's pace as nightfall grew darker. With pelting rain stinging our eyes and almost no light to guide us, we were practically navigating blind.

An hour and a half passed. I shifted in my seat, blew warm air into my hands, rubbed my palms against the denim clinging to my legs—yet there was nothing I could do to find comfort. Water ran down every inch of my skin, through every crack and crevice on my body. I shivered and quaked, teeth chattering despite my clenched and aching jaw. Finally I began to weep, little thin rivulets of tears washed away from my cheeks by the downpour. But since it did nothing to relieve my suffering, I ceased crying just as abruptly as I'd started. I recalled how I'd once fallen into a hill of red ants; how I'd burned my bare feet walking across a sheet of metal roofing out at the town dump in the middle of last summer; how I'd been beaned by a fastball right in the temple during a baseball game earlier that very month—and this was before helmets were used. But nothing could compare to the discomfort I felt at that moment. I gritted my teeth and searched in vain for the truck, interrupting my watch only to bail water out of the boat with the now-empty bait box.

Suddenly, without a word, my grandfather killed the engine. We continued to drift, the boat slowly rotating in the current, and all we could hear was water, driving down from above and rushing below, surrounding us completely. The sound of water had been mere background noise to the purr of the motor. Now, hearing it so clearly was terrifying.

I slid around in my seat. Grandpa looked from right to left and back, straining to see into the darkness.

"Doesn't make any sense," he muttered, frowning. "Where the hell—I'm disoriented, Henry. I know we should be nearing town, but the river doesn't look right to me. Can you see the truck? Look downriver!"

I saw nothing but a black void behind a sheet of precipitation. Did he really think I'd be able to make out something in the gloom that he couldn't see?

No, wait. Was the river this wide before? I wondered. *Are my eyes playing tricks on me in the night?*

"I think I see . . . the lake?" I said, confused.

My grandfather squinted and leaned forward. Then he gasped, his eyes and mouth opening wide. In a single motion he fell back onto his bench and grabbed the engine cord.

"Holy hell!" he shouted, starting the motor. "The river's overflowed the banks, and the lake must have crawled up another two hundred feet!"

The boat leaned as it tightly spun around, and I threw out my hands, grabbing the bow to keep from being flung out. Grandpa throttled the engine, no longer concerned with keeping our speed down in the now-widened river. We raced back upstream, staying tight to the western bank—or, at least, tight to where the bank used to be.

"Keep an eye out for the truck," he shouted. "We must have passed it a while ago and not even realized!" I leaned forward, peering into the wild tempest.

And for the first time since I'd awoken, I remembered my mother. I wished for nothing more than to be at home with her, warm and dry and wrapped in a blanket. Yet as frightened as I was out in the storm, her worry must be tenfold. I knew it for certain.

I imagined her, lantern in hand, pacing the house in a panic. I imagined her staring out the window, searching for the headlights of the truck, but seeing only her own eerie reflection in the black, rain-spotted panes. She paces again, looks at the clock, listens to the downpour throttling the house. Then she returns to the window by the front door; she looks out as lightning flashes, and where in past times she'd watched her husband and son coming home through the yard, she instead sees the surging waves of a swelling lake, climbing the porch steps like an unwanted visitor.

Though my imagination was immersed in the horrors my poor mother must have been experiencing, my subconscious mind had kept vigilant watch—and suddenly, I heard myself shouting, "*There's the truck!*" I came out of my dream, and my lonely mom was once again on her own.

We gunned toward the truck. When we approached within sixty or seventy feet of it, my grandfather cut the outboard motor and tipped it up out of the water to prevent the propeller from bottoming out.

Then we confirmed with our own eyes exactly what we'd feared: the dry land we'd left the truck sitting on was now beneath the flooded river—and would soon be part of the lake. Grandpa grabbed an oar and began to paddle the boat like a canoe. "Grab the other oar, Henry, and give me a hand," he shouted through the rain, his voice beginning to shake.

We paddled up to the truck and my grandfather leaped out into rushing water, clutching the tie-off rope so that I wouldn't drift away by my lonesome. The thunder and lightning had passed to the south, but the rain still fell steadily.

"The water's up to the running boards," he said with a sigh, "but it hasn't reached the engine yet. I think I can get it to start. Just hope I can get it to move."

He walked around to the back of the truck and towed the dinghy like a child with a toy sailboat on a string. He stumbled and nearly collapsed as the river surged around his calves.

"I don't think I can lift the boat into the back of the truck, so I'm going to tie it up to the bumper." His chest heaved with exhaustion as he struggled to catch his breath. "You wait, and I'll carry you into the cab of the truck. Then we'll get the hell out of here!"

•

Rainfall in the desert occurs rarely, for sure. Months often pass with nary a drop of precipitation. But when it comes, it comes *hard*. For nearly two hours we had endured exposure to one of the most hellish, unmerciful storms I've ever witnessed in my life.

In the cab of the truck, it felt like a blessing to be under cover at last. Shuddering and dripping, we sat and stared blankly at the dashboard, hypnotized by the sounds of our heavy panting and the pounding of rain on steel. I was too exhausted to speak or move, but after a moment, my grandfather turned stiffly, groaning in pain, and pulled a black, greasy rag out from behind his seat.

"Here," he ordered, "take this and try to dry yourself off a little bit."

I pressed the oil-soaked rag to my face, inhaling briefly, which gave me a slight headrush. I dabbed my forehead, neck, and arms, and handed the towel back over. Despite the grave situation, Grandpa chuckled when he saw the black streaks across my skin, as well as what was surely the most pathetic expression ever to adorn my face.

"Truck's running smoothly," he announced. I hadn't even noticed that he'd gotten it to turn over. Then he released the clutch and shifted. I held my breath.

Grandpa breathed deeply. "If we get stuck here, Henry—"

But the truck lurched forward, just an inch or so, and came to a stop. Then, as my grandfather lightly depressed the accelerator, we pitched forward again. It was slow and sluggish, but somehow we were driving through the river, towing our rowboat.

"*Ha ha!*" laughed my grandfather triumphantly. "We're going to make it!"

Minutes later we reached the edge of the water and pulled onto the surrounding muck, where we came to a stop. Without a word, Grandpa flung his door open and raced to the back of the truck. The adrenaline must have given him a burst of energy, because he hoisted the boat as if it were a cardboard box and heaved into the truck bed. Oars and fishing gear went flying and scattered beneath the hull. A moment later he was sitting beside me, his eyes wild below the matted salt-and-pepper hair pasted to his wrinkled forehead.

"We're going to take a higher-elevation route back home, which means we're going to be heading north a bit into the desert. Then we're going to hook left onto Salt Mine Road and drive back toward town as far as we can go."

"F-f-fine, Grandpa," I agreed with a thin, shaky voice.

"Let's go see your mother."

16.

O ur old house sat on the northern edge of town, two blocks east of where Route 91 intersected Salt Mine Road, the only road that ran due north out of town. If we couldn't drive all the way to our house—and I'm certain neither of us truly believed we could, at that point—then that meant the entire town would be flooded.

Sure enough, our home was now surrounded by lake water, which extended well past the north wall of the house by eighty to one hundred feet. Considering that it had just crept into the schoolyard across the street from our south-facing front door that very afternoon, we struggled to believe our own eyes. Grandpa and I glanced at each other, each of us with an incredulous look on his face that said, "Are you seeing this too, or am I going crazy?"

Back into the boat we went—but not until after a long slog through the still-falling rain. Despite our successful escape from the river, Grandpa was not interested in pushing our luck any further, opting to park the truck on Salt Mine Road more than a hundred feet from the water's edge. Every bone in my body ached, and I felt certain that I'd soon die of pneumonia or hypothermia. But I hoisted the dinghy with my grandfather and we marched through the downpour without once pausing to rest. Then we dumped the boat in the gritty mud and shoved off for the short trip home.

•

With Grandpa manning the oars, we darted around the house and floated up to the front porch in minutes. Water washed up above the top step, mere centimeters from breaching the porch itself.

I grabbed the rope and leaned forward to tie up to a column. As I tightened the double knot, the boat rocked violently, and I turned to see my grandfather jumping out and splashing up the inundated steps. He then leaned over the railing, plucked me up by my armpits, and set me down at the threshold of the front door.

"Go ahead, open it," he said before I even had a chance to reach for the knob. "What are you waiting for?"

We walked inside. Though it would be my home for only a short while longer, I'd never in my life been so glad to see it.

"We're home," said my grandfather in a loud, fatigued voice. "Henry, let's go upstairs, dry off, and get changed."

Weak and sniffling, we climbed the stairs. And as we ascended, I looked to my left into the parlor. On the coffee table, an oil lantern, barely burning, dimly lit the room. But I could still see boxes packed with books from the nearly empty shelves, along with a few pieces of antique luggage sitting on the lavender camelback sofa. One was zipped shut and bulged in the middle. Another was empty. The third was open, half-packed, and I could see several articles of my mother's clothing neatly folded and stacked within.

I entered my room. It was pitch dark, but I hardly noticed or cared since I'd been squinting through blackness all night long. I did not bother to shut the door as I peeled off my clothes, which hit the floor with a wet splat, like a soaked towel in a gym locker room. I didn't even take the time to pat myself dry, as I so eagerly wanted to dress myself in warm garments.

My mother had already packed about half of my clothes, but thankfully in the bottom of my dresser drawer I found a red flannel union suit, typically worn only on cold winter nights. I practically jumped into it, racing to button it up all the way to the neck. Then I pulled on a wool sweater and a pair of wool socks.

Instantly, a feeling of warmth spread through my whole body, from my toes to my scalp. It was so wonderful, so all-encompassing, I thought I might weep tears of joy. Instead, I sat at the edge of my bed, on top of my pillow, and placed my head in my hands. My bed beckoned to me to curl up and cocoon for ten or twelve hours, but I knew it would be impolite to fall asleep without first greeting my mother, so I resolved to summon the strength necessary to walk downstairs once more before bedtime.

Just then, I heard the heavy footfalls of my grandfather across the hallway. With his slow, lumbering gait, he often sounded like Frankenstein's monster thudding across the upstairs floorboards—and after the night we'd had, he sounded even more belabored and stiff than usual.

He arrived at the bottom of the stairs as I finally arose from my bed to follow him.

"Ellen," he said. I could hear him walking through the parlor toward the kitchen.

As I started down the stairs, I thought how odd it was that Mom hadn't come upstairs to see us—especially to see me, after I'd been out in the freezing rain for about a thousand hours. I thought she'd be upstairs in a flash to check on my wellbeing; instead, it seemed, she'd simply opted to keep packing her suitcases in preparation for the impending move.

"Ellen," came my grandfather's voice again. "Ellen?" He paused.

"Ellen!"

17.

"**W**HAT IS IT?" I asked, racing into the kitchen. "What's wrong with Mom?"

"I don't know, boy," said my grandpa. He clutched a lantern in his left hand and held it beneath his chin like he was telling a scary story by a campfire. "I can't find her!"

"What do you mean?" I yelled. "She's not *down here?*"

"*Not that I can see!*" he shouted in an even louder voice, as if we were engaged in a contest of decibels. "Grab the lantern in the parlor and go back upstairs—check all the closets in all the rooms and look under the beds. I didn't see her in her bedroom, but double-check there first."

"Okay—but where are you gonna check?"

"I'm going to run through this floor again, and if I don't find her, I'm going to check the backyard."

"But it's flooded!"

"*I know that!*"

All the pain in my joints had been forgotten; all the icy chills in my body melted away. I raced up the stairs, two at a time, and threw myself to the floor of my parents' room. I yanked up the fringe of the lacy bedskirt, thrust the lantern underneath, and came face to face . . . with absolutely nothing. Only dust.

I jumped to my feet.

"*Mom! Where are you, Mom?*"

I threw open the closet door. I rifled through dresses, overalls, flannels, pajamas, and stacks of small boxes. Then I dived blindly into the mess and tunneled as if I were a mole, digging and flinging clothing and cardboard out into the room. I was fortunate that I didn't knock over the oil lantern and meet a fate identical to that of my aunt and grandparents.

I could smell the faint scent of my mother and I swore could feel her there, caressing me gently, trying to calm me. But it was just the smell and sensation of the fabric of her garments. There was no one else in the closet. Just me.

I checked Grandpa's room in a similar manner—nothing. I tore apart my own room, peering into even the most ludicrous and impossible hiding spots, such as under my dresser, which not even a small child could fit beneath. And I ran the circuit three times over, until I was certain beyond a shadow of a doubt that my mother, Ellen Lord, was not on the second floor of the house. Of that I could be sure.

Bounding down the stairs, I shouted at the top of my lungs, "*Mom! Mom! Grandpa, I can't find Mom!*" Nobody answered. I turned to the right, glanced into the parlor, and then darted in the opposite direction into the dining room. I looked beneath the table and checked all the corners of the room. Finding it empty I continued into the kitchen.

I couldn't believe it. Now my grandfather had vanished too.

Then, suddenly, the back door burst open and my grandfather, once again drenched, waded up out of the lake and into the pantry.

"I can't find her out there, Henry," he said, wheezing and gasping, "and we're missing a lantern. She must have panicked and set out looking for us when we didn't return. She's out there *somewhere*, and I've got to go find her!"

He ran into the house and charged up the stairs. I followed him up, slipping on the puddles he left behind.

"I'm going too!" I asserted.

"The *hell you are!*" he shouted, emerging from his room with an old rain slicker. "No, you're staying right here!"

My face flushed and twisted with rage, and I tried to conjure words of protest but couldn't.

"Don't even *think* about stepping outside this house tonight!" he ordered as he thundered down the stairs. "You hear me? Don't you *move*! I'll be back in a while. Come hell or high water, I'm going to find Ellen!"

And then he trudged out onto the front porch and slammed the door. I watched through the window as he untied the boat and shoved off, paddling with all his remaining might around the house in the direction of the truck to retrieve the outboard motor. Minutes later I heard the engine roar. The buzz of the Evinrude cut through the night, becoming fainter and then fading entirely as Grandpa disappeared to the east.

Then I was alone in the dark house. The rain had slowed to a soft patter, and it was the only noise I could hear other than the loud ringing in my ears. Then, even though I couldn't remember when I'd last eaten, I doubled over and heaved and vomited until I collapsed. I bawled out of despair, rage, and unimaginable pain, in that order. Through blinding tears I tried my hand at prayer, desperately imagining something to offer, something I could sacrifice in exchange for the safe return of my mother. But how can you bargain or barter when you've nothing left to give?

Eventually, at long last, I lost consciousness on the floor at the base of the staircase.

18.

I WOKE UP the next morning in my own bed, tucked in tightly beneath the covers. My face had been washed, but I still wore my winter pajamas, as well as the wool sweater. And with the temperature already rising with the sun, I had become sticky with sweat.

As I was coming to, for just a brief, glorious fraction of a second, all was well in the world. I was in my familiar old bed in my familiar old bedroom where I'd fallen asleep every night and awoken every morning of my life. My feet were scrunched against the mahogany footboards, and all across my room the sun spread shivery shadows of the leaves of the cottonwood tree in our front yard. It was, for a brief, glorious fraction of a second, a morning just like any other morning that had preceded it.

Sadly, the dam in the mind that holds back consciousness during sleep burst wide open, flooding me with images and recollections of the previous night. I tore off the blankets as if they were on fire and pulled the sweater over my head as I jumped out of bed. Struggling to get the sweater off, I blindly dashed out of my bedroom and into my mother's.

"*Mom?*" I called out, finally freeing myself of the pullover.

Her bed was neatly made except for a few wrinkles I'd put in the crocheted quilt the prior evening while searching beneath the bed frame. Boxes, shoes, and articles of clothes belonging to both my parents were strewn about, spilling out of the open closet. The room was just as I'd left it. Next door, Grandpa's bed was also untouched, though a second set of sopping wet clothes sat on the floor beside the ones he'd changed out of after we'd first arrived home from our river adventure.

I turned to go downstairs to locate my grandfather. I stopped when I noticed a note sitting on the top step: *Out looking for your mother. Taking the boat and checking all the buildings in town. May head up to Overton too. Eat something today. Drink lots of water too. Stay inside.*

Alone again. I didn't feel much like going downstairs, but I didn't want to stay upstairs either. Slowly, I trudged down and opened the front door at the foot of the steps.

Had it not been so tragic, I would have admired the odd beauty of what I saw. The whole town was immersed in the lake, the remaining buildings protruding out of the water, which licked at first-floor windows. With the storm now but a memory, the water glittered beneath the bright blue sky. Full-length shadows of trees and homes fell across gentle, breeze-blown currents.

Since last night, the lake had claimed our porch as well. It was just up to the base of the door and covered the porch floorboards with about a half-inch of water.

Flooding in the desert is normal. I'd grown accustomed to it, having lived my whole life there. Thanks to an unusually high water table beneath the very dry (and exceptionally thin) top layer of soil, the ground simply cannot absorb water rapidly enough. Look at Las Vegas—it receives, on average, less than five inches of rain in a full year, yet the city is veined with deep flood channels that would make New Orleans green with envy. Water builds up, flash floods occur, and even temporary lakes form on the otherwise dry playas. Yet within a day or so, it's as if the rain had never fallen.

But what I saw here was not going anywhere. This lake was forever, and despite the utter absence of rainclouds in the sky, it would only get worse, as the Virgin, Muddy, and Colorado Rivers continued to dump water into Lake Mead at a rate of thousands of gallons per second.

I pulled the cuffs of my union suit up to my calves and stepped out barefooted. The water was cold enough to cause a twinge to shoot up the backs of my legs, but I shuffled over to the edge of the porch at the western corner of the house, leaned on the railing, and glanced around the side of the building.

I already knew how it would be. But seeing the water fully covering the foundation window by at least a foot drove home the reality for me: the crawl-space beneath the house was immersed.

I didn't even entertain the notion that I might be able to swim underneath and rescue the items. The safe was situated far back beneath the concrete slab of the first floor, nearly equidistant from the windows on both the eastern and western faces of the home. Besides, even if I could get down there and hold my breath long enough, I'd never be able to see the combination lock without the light of a lantern. So I just stood there, leaning on the railing, letting it sink in.

"I keep some of the most important things I have in here."

My father's safe was permanently entombed in Lake Mead.

"No matter what happens, it will all be secure down here."

And though he'd been dead for three years, I had let him down.

"It's stuff that I want you to have someday."

As well as myself.

•

I meandered on the porch and slowly drifted back toward the door. Way off in the distance, the hum of a motor echoed over the lake. As I reached for the doorknob, I realized that the sound was drawing closer.

Suddenly, a few blocks down the street to the west, the boat shot out from behind an abandoned residence and banked left, heading in the direction of our house. Autos would no longer travel down this portion of Route 91, but Grandpa certainly seemed to be navigating it just fine in the dinghy. As he roared past his empty garage, I noticed that he wasn't alone—someone was in the boat with him, sitting in my usual seat up front in the bow. Hope stirred in my chest as I gulped a deep breath of air and held it in.

Grandpa then noticed me standing there. He called out over the cacophony of the motor and waved to me, motioning for me to stay put. Then he cut the engine, letting the boat's momentum carry its passengers right up to the front steps.

"Morning, Little Henry."

It was Whitmore, the old postman, who was riding passenger. He offered a small, polite smile but struggled to maintain eye contact. I don't think I could help the look of shock and disappointment that must have washed over my face when I saw him instead of my mother—and I'm sure he recognized it as such.

"Good morning, sir," I said with a raspy, weary voice.

"Morning, Henry," echoed my grandfather as the bow slowly passed by and he arrived at my side in the stern. Grandpa leaned over slightly and grabbed a porch column, halting the rowboat. His eyes were sunken and red, with dark bags hanging beneath them, and the corners of his mouth trembled.

He let out a long sigh.

"Well," he started. His voice faded and the word hung in the air a moment. He stared ahead blankly, as if he were watching it suspended in front of his face like a helium balloon while he contemplated what to say. "Well, I went up the Muddy again last night in the rain. I hugged the shoreline for a good five miles looking for any sign of your mom or anyone else who might've gotten trapped out there. I was out there until probably—I don't know, three in the morning, I'd say.

"When I got back, I put you to bed and changed my clothes. Then I woke up Mr. Whitmore here, since I knew he was still in town—he's the *last* one, actually. You know, aside from us. Anyhow, we went through town calling for your mother. I thought maybe she'd gone out and gotten trapped by the storm; maybe took shelter somewhere. And when the sun came up and we still hadn't found her, we entered every single building in town. Searched 'em top to bottom."

I thought he was going to keep talking, but he'd trailed off once again and left a gap of silence to be filled. So I asked, "And?"

"Nothing," he replied. "We didn't find anyone at all. So," he said, exhaling deeply and refocusing his thoughts, "now we're heading back to the truck. It's parked out where we left it last night, so I'm gonna pull the boat up there and drive up into Overton for a bit. We'll go through town and ask around, see if anyone has seen her. I'm hoping that maybe last night when the rain came she hitched on with someone else heading for higher ground. We'll see."

"Can I come?" I asked hopefully.

"Sorry, boy," said Grandpa, shaking his head. "I want you to keep a watch out here."

I couldn't bring myself to look at my grandfather. I nodded with downcast eyes, gazing at my legs where they met the surface of the water.

"Hey. Look at me when I'm talking to you," he snapped. I made eye contact immediately. "She might come back at some point, and if she does, I want you to be here, because she might need a hand.

"I love you," he said, "and I'll be back soon."

Then he let go of the column, pulled the engine cord, and took off around the side of the house and was gone.

•

It was several minutes before nine o'clock in the morning when Grandpa and Whitmore left me behind. I had the entire day ahead of me to pass in the house that had become my cell, and the idea made me feel physically sick. My head throbbed, my stomach ached from my guts to my throat, and my whole body shivered, even though it was a typical blazing hot morning.

Inside, I dried off my feet and walked to the kitchen to sip a glass of water. I could feel the liquid all the way from my tongue to my throat to the burning pit of my stomach, where it mixed with bile and acid. I felt like it was coming back up, but miraculously I kept it down.

There was no way I was going to eat. I hadn't any appetite anyway.

I shuffled back through the living room, trying to avert my stare from the luggage on the sofa and the books neatly packed in boxes on the floor. I sat down on the staircase, on the third or fourth step, and looked out the window in the parlor to my right. Then I looked out the dining room window to my left.

I spent most of the day there, sitting and waiting. I may have dozed off a few times as I rested my head in my hands and my elbows on my knees. The day went by at high speed and in slow motion at the same time. It seemed endless while it was passing, and when it was over, it felt like a dream, as if it hadn't even happened at all.

In the early evening, my grandfather came in through the back door and entered the kitchen to fill his canteen and eat a bite of food. I padded softly through the dining room and saw him as he was taking a bite out of a hunk of bread. He was alone now, and when he saw me, his expression told me everything I needed to know about his day. He looked weather-beaten and ancient—the past twenty-four hours had aged him decades.

He came toward me without a word, hugged me tightly, and patted my back as he turned to leave. He stepped out the back door directly into the boat.

•

Later, from my bedroom, I took a last look at my town. Far too little of it remained. But the sunset remained the same as ever, burning the sky as it sank into the Valley of Fire. Nearly every color I'd ever seen in my life faded in and out, passing through every existing hue of red and orange, pink and purple, blue and black. It was a spectacular show, and long after darkness had fallen and the Milky Way had come out of hiding, I lay down in my bed.

They may have higher ground elsewhere, I thought, *but there isn't any other place on Earth where you can get a show like that.* At that time, I didn't have any basis of comparison. But it's true. There isn't.

19.

"WAKE UP, boy. It's time to go. We have to get out of here now."

I awoke, gagging. Grandpa stood beside my bed, reeking of gasoline and dressed in the same clothes he'd been wearing since the previous morning. He was a mechanic; I was used to the smell—but it was overpowering, and seemingly not coming just from his clothes and skin. A breeze blew in from outside, and I noticed through my watery eyes that the windows were wide open.

"What's going on?" I asked as I slowly pulled the blankets back. "What's with the smell?"

"Get dressed," ordered my grandfather, "and pack what you want to take with you in your bag." He motioned to the old Gladstone that my mom had partially filled with clothes two days prior. "Meet me downstairs. And hurry up."

He exited the room and stomped down the stairs as I swung my legs out of bed. Finally, my sleep-addled mind recognized that the smell of gas was coming from the house. Wet, runny stains were splattered on the walls, and trails of gasoline crisscrossed the floors from my room out to the hallways and into the other two bedrooms. I was feeling sicker to my stomach with each passing moment, so I grabbed my bag, threw a couple more shirts into it, and rushed into my parents' room.

The bedroom was still in disarray, though it appeared that my grandfather had picked through it some. The bedspread was gone, the framed photo and desert sky painting had vanished from the walls, and knick-knacks that had sat on the two matching dressers were gone as well. There was one thing I was certain he hadn't found though—so once again, I tore into the closet, this time with the aid of the sun to light the way. And there, far in the back on a shelf, I found my dad's old, dried-out Hutch baseball glove. I stuffed it in my bag, wrapping it in a collared shirt. And as I walked out, I snatched my mother's pewter jewelry box, which sat open and empty on her otherwise bare nightstand.

I was still groggy, and the gas fumes were not helping. Slowly, I staggered down the steps, not even bothering to take another glance into my bedroom. At the bottom of the stairs, rather than walking out the wide-open front door, I turned and stepped into the living room.

The entire downstairs was flooded with water. During the night, the lake had quietly crept into the house like a burglar; now there was ankle-deep standing water throughout the entire first floor.

Seeing the lake approaching our property and later fully surrounding the house had been difficult, but now, the finality of the situation hit me full force. I began to panic with the realization that this was it. The end had arrived.

Since then, I've had other moments like that in my life, where I've prepared myself for a difficult, life-altering event by building a false façade of bravery and a phony pretense of acceptance—even anticipation. It's what just about everyone does when, for example, a beloved family member is terminally ill. "It's for the best," you tell yourself as death makes its grueling approach. "She's suffering so terribly, and I just don't want her to go through this any longer." And then she dies, and her sudden liberty from pain is hardly consolation for the hurt and heartache that you've abruptly inherited.

For many months I'd secretly wished that we could leave St. Thomas. I was so tired of the stubborn ways of my mother and, even more so, of my grandfather. I knew the time to move would come eventually, and I knew that it would happen whether we left when the lake was still hundreds of feet away or when it was claiming our home by force. But I'd wanted it to happen sooner rather than later; I wanted the lake to tie our whole town to a tree and smack it with a shovel. *Just get it over with.* I couldn't take the waiting because, foolishly, I thought the waiting was worse than the final act.

But I'd learned my lesson. As I stood there, turning in circles in the water surging through our home, I wanted to stay there for the rest of my life. Everything I yearned for was right there within those four walls, and it was being irrevocably ripped away from me.

"Henry!" my grandfather called out suddenly. He was on the porch in a pair of waders, looking at me with impatience through the open doorway. "Get out here and get in the boat. We're leaving."

In a daze, I looked around for the luggage and the boxes of books my mother had left around the parlor, but they were gone.

"If you're looking for shoes, I've got a pair in the dinghy for you," said Grandpa. I sloshed out to join him, and he guided me directly into the boat.

"Where's all of our stuff?" I asked as he untied the rope from the porch rail. "Where did the boxes and bags go?"

"I packed as much of it as I could into the truck during the night. I took about five trips with the boat to the truck and then drove into Overton to unload the heavier items. I got the most important things. We can just buy new furniture."

The boat now loosed from the porch, Grandpa squatted and landed with a thump on the middle bench seat, facing me. He pushed off from the railing, and instead of directing me to pull the cord to start the outboard motor, he grabbed the oars and began to paddle. We rowed through the shadow of the big old cottonwood, which had sprouted remarkably full leaves since the lake water had saturated its thirsty roots.

I was still perplexed. "So where in Overton did you leave everything?"

"Oh," he responded as we looped back behind the house and drifted beneath the open kitchen window. "I bought a house yesterday up in town."

He reached into the hip pocket of his blue jeans and produced a paper matchbook.

"Yep, it's a nice place."

Then he pulled out a match and struck it on the zipper of his blue jeans, as he often did.

"I think you'll like it."

Then he touched the flame to the heads of the other matches. A flare leaped up in his fingertips, and he tossed the whole book through the window where it landed out of sight on the countertop.

At once, flames roared up into view and rapidly spread through the entire kitchen. I was amazed at how instantly searing it felt, even though Grandpa had begun to row frantically the moment he'd released the matchbook, distancing us from the burgeoning inferno.

I couldn't see it, but I knew that the fire was tearing through the house—along the walls, across the bookshelves, and up the stairs. Only minutes earlier, I'd had my head buried in a pillow in my room; now my room was enflamed. In another few minutes our home would exist only in my memory, placed on a shelf in the back of my mind alongside my mother and father, the farms and streets and homes, and the sunsets and moonrises of old St. Thomas.

•

Rather than parking north of the house on Salt Mine Road, Grandpa had parked the truck among the bluffs just beyond the northwest corner of town, out past Whitmore's former home. But with the effort he was expending, huffing and puffing as he stroked the oars with all his strength, it would take mere moments for the ride to be over.

And in the short amount of time it took us to glide across the flooded basin of the Moapa Valley, the blaze did its work apace.

Fire burrowed through the interior walls of the house and jumped out onto the clapboards. Flames seemed to be leaping right up out of the water as they hungrily devoured the home, charring it as if it were a massive briquette. Thick, dark ribbons of smoke began to pour from the upstairs windows, and just as the structure began to wobble and sway, our dinghy bottomed out at the base of the plateau where the truck sat.

"God damn it!"

Grandpa leaped out and dragged the boat to shore, furious and cursing, with me still inside. When he paused for a moment I jumped out to help, but he scrambled up the crumbly slope, dragging the dinghy behind him like a man suddenly imbued with the strength of five.

I followed, stumbling on the steep incline, and when I reached the top my grandfather grabbed my hands, yanked me off my feet, and set me down. Then we turned just in time to see the house cave in. The hot tinder hissed like a rattler when it touched down in the lake, and it spewed a dense, murky blossom of black steam and smoke that looked like the ash plume of an erupting volcano.

Stunned, I stood motionless until my grandfather patted my shoulders and gave them a squeeze.

"Let's get going so you can help me empty out the truck at home." He cleared his throat and swallowed hard, choking back tears. "Then we'll come back for the boat. Maybe we can go fishing this weekend."

20.

MY GRANDFATHER hadn't gotten a wink of sleep since I'd woken him in the boat more than fifty hours earlier as the rain began to fall. But he didn't rest until the entire truck had been emptied and the boat was sitting in our new front yard. We slept side by side on the wooden floor of the living room the first night, surrounded by boxes and bags, exhausted beyond all belief.

For such an impulsive, last-minute purchase, the home Grandpa had chosen was remarkably similar to the one he'd torched: a whitewashed two-story home with a gabled roof and cottonwoods in the yard to provide shade. But it was built of bricks, not wood, and it also had electricity and flush toilets, which until then had been a luxury that I'd enjoyed only at school.

There was no porch though, and no elevated foundation, which meant no crawlspace. The house sat on a flat concrete slab. I was glad. I felt that it would be a relief not to have a constant reminder that I'd forgotten to save my father's most treasured possessions.

•

Our new dwelling in Overton had only two bedrooms on the second level, not three like in our old home. This one had a third bedroom on the ground floor, which Grandpa took. I slept upstairs in the room to the left of the steps, just like in St. Thomas.

On the day we acquired the majority of our new furniture, including all of the new beds and nightstands, Grandpa vanished into the room across the hall from mine for several hours. For a long time he was quiet, and then I could hear him behind the closed door, grunting and dragging heavy furniture across the floor. When I turned the knob to enter and offer my assistance, I found that it had been locked.

I knocked.

"Need any help, Grandpa?"

"Nope," he replied. "All set in here."

So I waited, reading in my newly furnished room, feeling princely as I held my book beneath the artificial light of the electric lamp on my nightstand, even though natural daylight would've sufficed. Finally, I heard the opening of the door across the hall, so I set off to see what my grandfather had done.

He stood back from the door admiring his work. I squeezed past him and entered the room.

Grandpa had created a near-perfect replica of the bedroom once occupied by his son and daughter-in-law. The painting and my baby photo hung just as they had before, in roughly the same spots on the wall. The bed was positioned against the far wall, centered in the room, just as the old bed had been in the old house. My mother's crocheted bedspread covered the mattress, and the frilly lace of the bed skirt neatly dangled from the frame, brushing the floor.

At the head of the bed were two nightstands, one positioned on each side. On what would have been my mother's sat a small stack of hardcover books, a pair of necklaces, and a haphazard pile of costume jewelry; on my father's, a pocket watch rested atop a copy of the 1935 *Farmers' Almanac*, and his old navy blue woolen cap hung from the bedpost.

Hanging inside the open closet were several shirts, trousers, skirts, and sweaters that had belonged to my parents. One of my mother's favorite white cotton sundresses hung in the window, catching the afternoon sun, and a full set of clean work clothes that my father had worn to the garage was neatly folded and stacked at the foot of the bed.

"What do you think?" Grandpa asked.

I didn't know *what* to think, exactly. It was all at once beautiful and depressing, both a touching memorial to beloved family, and a heartbreaking, creepy shrine that eternalized the moments of my father's passing and my mother's disappearance. It wasn't the bedroom my parents had left behind, but one created specifically for them after they'd gone from our lives. A room waiting for occupants who would never arrive. I'd have to look into it whenever I walked to or from the staircase and face the feelings and memories it stirred within me every time.

"I think they'd like it," I said. I left it at that.

•

At the time that my grandfather assembled the bedroom, we still didn't know for certain whether my mother was alive or dead. At that time she had only been missing for about a week, and we held tight to a tacit hope that she would someday return. And when she did, her bedroom would be waiting for her.

Of course, she did not come back.

In late September of 1938, we drove out to the bluff we'd scrambled atop three and a half months earlier to witness our flaming home collapse. By this time the top of the plateau had become the shore of Lake Mead, which had swallowed all but the tops of the tallest trees and the apexes of the highest remaining buildings.

We stood in silence. It was an awkward, informal, irreligious sort of funeral. There were no words of mourning, no black veils, no bouquets of roses. There were no priests nor preachers, no prayers, no pallbearers, no taps. But standing there in the dust, casually dressed in jeans and t-shirts, we finally had our funerary moment of closure.

We may not have known the exact circumstances

of her death, but of this we were certain: the remains of my mother rested somewhere in the dark trenches of Lake Mead. Its waters would always be a tomb in our eyes.

•

That same month, September of 1938, I started seventh grade, returning to the school in Overton—though now my walk was much, much shorter, as our house was less than a half-mile down the road. My days of waiting for rides and enduring endless marches through the desert when no one showed up were over.

That fall, Grandpa and I began to take the dinghy out again too. The waters of both the Muddy and Virgin Rivers had dropped to levels far too low to accommodate even our little boat, so we spent our time floating in the relatively new Bowman Reservoir, created two years earlier when the Wells Siding Diversion Dam was put up by the Civilian Conservation Corps. I liked their work—it hadn't wrecked any lives or livelihoods, and the reservoir was peaceful, calm, and loaded with fish for my grandfather. Plus, being only a fraction of the size of Lake Mead, it never attracted a crowd. We went out when we could, but not nearly as frequently as when we'd lived in St. Thomas.

The reason we had less time for boating was that my grandfather had opened a new service station on Route 12, several blocks north of our home, within weeks of arriving in Overton. Most of his old St.

Thomas customers had relocated to Logandale and Overton, and many returned for his services now that his new shop was conveniently located. With the relatively large population and the influx of tourists heading from Salt Lake City to Valley of Fire—plus the fact that with every passing year, more people were buying automobiles—Grandpa's shop became busier than ever. He hired an assistant in November of 1938, and a second employee several months later. By 1940 he had a team of four mechanics working for him, and his shop expanded to house three bays.

Eventually, in early 1942, he took on a fifth assistant, as well as a definite successor to take over the business—at least, that was how he saw it. Grandpa taught me everything he could about auto repair and maintenance. I got lessons in clutch repair, oil and transmission fluid replacement, drum brake reassembly, coolant flushing—you name it. I learned it all, and I became somewhat of a fixture down at the shop during summer breaks and weekends. The men who came in and rustled my hair when I was a toddler hiding in the back corner of the garage in St. Thomas now came to me for tire patches and wheel alignments.

I enjoyed working with my grandfather, and he enjoyed working with me. We were the only family we each had left, but we genuinely liked each other's company—and most of the time we spent together was spent at the garage.

"You're a good, hard worker, boy," he'd say to me. "A little bit slow, but that's just because you *think* too much. You'll do a fine job when you take over the business someday."

I'd nod and smile awkwardly to mask my guilt, wishing that I had the ambition to follow in his footsteps but knowing that I did not.

•

I did have the ambition to follow in the footsteps of someone in my family—but it wasn't my grandfather.

I was an avid reader and an excellent student, as I knew my mother had been, and I owed a lot to the early years of home schooling in the parlor where I'd been her sole student. I figured that I might be able to take after her and do for other kids what she'd done for me. Before I even entered high school, I decided I'd like to become a teacher—maybe even go to college. Mom didn't have a chance to attend a university, and worse yet, she taught in a classroom for only five short years before that career was taken from her—a pitiful misfortune that became a permanent tragedy. In a way, I felt I *had* to do it for her. But it had to be somewhere else.

Reading so much from a young age had turned me into a prodigious armchair explorer. In my imagination I had traveled the world over, though in actuality I'd never left the Moapa Valley, other than a day-trip to Las Vegas in '39 on the Los Angeles and Salt Lake Railroad. Like many young people before me and since, I sought a chance to journey outside of my hometown and see these places (or at least *some* of them) with my own eyes. The desert would always be a home I could return to, I thought, so long as Grandpa stayed here.

The years spent peppering the side of the St. Thomas Schoolhouse with baseballs had paid some dividends as well: I had a great arm and was one of the best pitchers in Clark County. I was nifty with the glove too, switching between shortstop and center field when I wasn't on the mound. Even my bat was decent, despite the fact that I hadn't really learned to hit until I was nearing my tenth birthday. I wanted to keep playing after high school ended, and that wasn't an option if I stayed in Nevada.

21.

IT WASN'T UNTIL the spring of 1943, near the end of my junior year of high school, that I finally informed Grandpa of my plans. For years the idea of leaving home had festered in me, but the more I dwelled on it, the harder I thought my grandfather would take the news. I didn't want to hurt his feelings, but I couldn't let my plans slide either.

Finally, I told him that I wanted to go to college and become a teacher. I had my sights set on Eastern Montana State Normal School, a small teacher's college up in Billings. I'd dreamed of going to Big Sky Country since my mother had read aloud to me the journals of Lewis and Clark, and going to this college would let me explore some of the places they'd so vividly described. Plus, the school had a baseball team, the Yellow Jackets, and I was sure I could make it onto the squad as a pitcher.

"Hm," said my grandfather. We were sitting at the dining table, eating a late dinner of canned soup. After school I'd stayed at the garage until well after dark, helping him and the crew get caught up on the backlog of work to be done. He didn't take his eyes off his spoon as he lifted it to his mouth to take another loud slurp. Then he set it down, leaned forward, and stared me down, as he always did in serious conversation.

"You know, I've been planning to turn over the shop to you, Henry," he said, as if it were the first time he were telling me and not the hundredth.

"Yeah, I know, Grandpa."

"There's good money to be made. Good money. I've made a bundle over the years, and I'll bet you'd do even better, considering how well-liked you are around here."

"Oh, I don't know about that," I replied, doing my best to flatter him and deflect attention from myself. "You're about the best-loved mechanic in the country. Think about how everyone comes from all over to visit your garage! You know, I'll bet that there's no other place in the world where a garage is as—"

"Save it." I stopped talking and fidgeted in my seat. "I'm disappointed that you want to leave. I always thought we'd work together when you graduated. It was something I was looking forward to."

And I'd been afraid of breaking *his* heart. My own felt as if it were shattering, and my stomach tied itself in knots as I frantically searched my mind for the most tactful words to take it all back.

"But," he continued, "I always did have a feeling this would happen. You're a smart kid, and you're a lot more like your mom than you are like me."

"Really?" I said, blinking back the tears of guilt I'd almost let fall from my eyes.

"Sure. As I always say, you're a hard worker, but I know you've got your own ideas about the things you want to do. I'm not going to get in the way. Besides," he added with an almost undetectable smirk, "you'll be coming home during the summers, whether you like it or not. I can't get through the busy season at the garage without you."

"You bet," I blurted out, more relieved that my guilt had been absolved than at the fact that I'd be allowed to go to college. "I'll be back every summer, every Christmas break, and maybe I'll even move back right after graduation, and maybe we'll run the garage together after all. You never know, right?"

"Yeah, right, but don't get too far ahead of yourself," he said, picking up his soupspoon to indicate that the conversation had run its course. "You've got a lot of time to figure that out. Worry about it when the time comes."

•

It was settled: I'd go to college in Montana. I enrolled to start classes in the autumn semester of 1944 and would make the trip by train—I'd ride up to Ogden, Utah from Overton and then head to Cheyenne, Wyoming. From Cheyenne I'd make the long trip north to Billings on a line that would make no less than twenty stops along the way. It would be a great adventure, I thought, and I spent most of the summer following my high school graduation in a restless state, both eager to start my journey and apprehensive to leave home.

The date of my departure drew near. And though the summer heat reached temperatures that any sane person would consider unsuitable for recreation, Grandpa and I couldn't resist the opportunity for one last ride around the Bowman Reservoir in the dinghy. With my trip less than a week away, we dropped the boat in the water and went for a bittersweet, nostalgic spin.

Unfortunately, it was just too uncomfortable to be out in the open, and the light breeze did little to cool us down. Even when you've got the whole lake to yourself and there's not a soul within miles, boiling in your own skin is not especially peaceful, nor enjoyable. Nowadays, there are plenty of shady groves along the shore of the turquoise reservoir to the north of Logandale. Back then, there were not, so we left just as quickly as we'd arrived.

"Sorry, Henry," said my grandfather, quietly laughing as we drove back home. "That wasn't much fun."

"At least we tried," I said, staring ahead at the dusty road. My hands burned from touching the scorching aluminum siding of the boat. "We'll just have to wait until I come home in December."

"You know, I was thinking maybe I'd take a drive up to see you this fall," he said. Stunned, I turned to look at him, and he glanced sidelong at me. "What? You don't think I'd want to visit you and see what this school is all about? Maybe I can see some of these rivers and mountains you keep going on about—and watch you throw some pitches too. I've hardly missed one of your games yet."

I didn't want to risk discouraging him with the news that baseball wouldn't start until spring, so I let it slide. "That would be great," I said. "Maybe you can make it up before Thanksgiving, and then I can come back to Nevada with you for the holidays. We can take a road trip together and visit Yellowstone—"

"Now you're talking," he interjected. "You know, I always wanted to go there."

"Me too," I agreed as we pulled into the driveway and came to a stop.

Grandpa parked the truck in the shade and killed the ignition. Then he reached over with an open palm, whacked me on the shoulder, and squeezed it tight. "I have to say, I was pretty upset about you leaving, and I'm gonna miss you, boy. But I'm excited about all this. It's giving me a lot to look forward to. They say that's what helps you live a long life."

"That and keeping busy," I added.

"Sure, sure, and I've already got plenty to do down at the garage. At this rate, I'll live to be a hundred and fifty."

We had a good laugh at that and then retreated inside. It was stifling in the house though, and since it was still early afternoon, we headed down to the garage to help out the weekend crew.

•

Shortly before four o'clock in the afternoon, my grandfather, still in high spirits, sent everyone home early. Jones was in the grease pit beneath a pickup, and Evans was hunched under the hood of a Packard, overhauling a carburetor. Still, they dropped what they were doing without delay and slipped out the door, knowing that it may be the only time that Henry Lord would send them home early.

"Enjoy the rest of the afternoon," he called after, slinging a blotchy rag over his shoulder. Then he searched around like a puzzled dog until finally he found me crawling under the truck to take over the oil change.

"You too, Henry. Get lost. Go home and start packing. I can take over from here."

"When are you coming home?" I grunted as I slid out of the pit.

"Oh, I don't know. Earlier rather than later, I hope. But I'm going to do what needs to be done, so go ahead and have dinner without me if you get tired of waiting."

Pardoned from responsibility, I walked swiftly to the door, eager to start packing my bags and to fantasize about the trip that was only six days away. "All right, then. See you in a bit," I shouted as I strode out the side door, letting it slam behind me.

"Okay," I heard him say. He may have added something else as the door banged shut, but I couldn't hear.

•

Like reading a great novel or having a conversation with an old friend, packing for a major trip is one of those activities where time seems to pick up steam and charge forward at an accelerated rate. Suddenly, you look up and discover that hours have passed like minutes, and you wonder how your mind, so alert and awake, has separated itself so fully from your body, which you haven't noticed is hungry, fatigued, and ready for sleep.

It was nearly ten o'clock when I finally checked the time. Though I'd completed the majority of my packing for the big move, I'd neglected to eat dinner and was famished. My grandfather was still burning the midnight oil too, and was probably just as hungry since we hadn't taken any food to the garage that afternoon.

I grabbed a couple pieces of fruit and threw them in a paper bag as I walked out, not even bothering to switch off the lights or lock the door since we'd be returning shortly.

When I arrived at the shop, the overhead doors were all shut, but the side door was propped open. My grandfather often left the door and a couple windows ajar after sunset to allow a nice cross-breeze to cool the place a bit.

I sauntered in, glad to see him. He was leaning into the engine compartment of the Packard, undoubtedly still tinkering with the carburetor.

"Hey, Grandpa," I shouted across the garage. There was no radio playing, nobody chattering out in the nearby street. My voice sounded deafening in the silent concrete room. "I brought you something to eat."

When he didn't respond, I knew. I knew immediately, and I knew absolutely. And what's funny is that the very first thought in my mind was, *What about our trip to Yellowstone? Couldn't you have just waited until after our trip to Yellowstone?* I felt ashamed for the notion, but I couldn't help it. It just popped into my head.

The bag of apples fell from my hand and I ran toward him, circling behind the truck that was between us. He was slumped facedown against the engine. His left arm splayed to the side while his right arm was curled beneath his torso, his fist loosely clutching his chest. I poked him once in the left kidney, jabbing hard with two fingers, and then I jumped back, terrified, as if he might spin around and shout "*BOO!*" But he just lay there like a cold sack of clay.

Though I'd lost both my parents, I had never before witnessed death or its aftermath. It was not the peaceful slumber that I'd been told about. Men at rest don't plant their cheeks on a gearbox, nor do they empty their bowels in their favorite pair of overalls. Men at rest eventually come awake, strong and spirited, to eat apples brought to them by their grandsons; dead men are impotent husks of inert, swollen flesh bruised by static blood. It frightened me to learn that it doesn't matter if you wake up feeling fine and healthy, go boating, and make grand future plans. You can end up a crumpled corpse under the hood of a roadster by bedtime.

The last of the Lords wept for the latest to fall. Then it occurred to me that I would be leaving the valley for good in less than a week. I now had a destination and no return ticket.

•

Grandpa had left behind a simple will with simple instructions: everything to me. In his 68 years, he'd somehow saved up more than $10,000 in his bank account despite the lean times in St. Thomas. I figured I had plenty to live on, so I turned over the garage to his employees on one condition: if I ever needed a job, at any time, they had to hire me on. They accepted the proposition with no arguments.

There was one other important item I had to give away before leaving town.

I pulled up into old Whitmore's driveway just before eight o'clock on August 19, 1944. It was a sunny, bright Saturday morning, but the coolness of the night still lingered, and Mr. Whitmore was sitting out on his porch rocker enjoying it.

"Hi, Mr. Whitmore," I called out from inside the truck. "Mind if I come up for just a moment?"

"Not at all, Henry," he said.

Whitmore had already paid his respects and offered his condolences when he'd dropped by the house the previous day. He regarded me curiously, wondering why I'd be stopping by to see him again so soon, and so early in the day.

"As I mentioned yesterday, I'm about to leave town," I began as I climbed the steps. "I was wondering if you might do me a big favor."

"Of course," the postman replied warmly. "What can I help you with?"

"I know you're retired, but I'd like to see if you might make one last delivery for me." I held out a small can. Inside of it were my grandpa's ashes.

"On your old route," I added.

He leaned forward in his rocking chair and gingerly took the container from my hands. He seemed to know just what I was handing to him.

"I'm glad to help, Henry," he said. "But I'm not sure I understand what you mean."

"You know my grandfather—he hated that lake more than anyone. But I think he'd probably like to go home, even if it means going for a short ride across Mead."

Whitmore looked at the can and then at me. Deep lines crossed his forehead, and there was concern in his eyes. "But what about you?" he asked. "Don't you want to be there to scatter his ashes?"

"I haven't been down to Mead since the year we got flooded out, and . . . I don't know. I'd just rather not go to another funeral at the lake. But," I finished, with a deep breath, "I'd really love for Grandpa to be put to rest where he lived most of his life. It just wouldn't seem right any other way."

Whitmore stuck out his hand and we shook in

agreement. "I'll make sure he gets there today," he said. He smiled broadly, and his eyes were wet.

"Oh, there's one more thing." I reached into my hip pocket and pulled out my train ticket to Billings. I tore it into tiny pieces and dropped it into the makeshift urn. Then I left the boat with Whitmore, said farewell, and went home to load up the truck. Before high noon I hit the road; two nights later I was camped out on the shore of Yellowstone Lake.

•

Lodgepole pines swayed overhead as I listened to the howls, shrieks, and cries of unimaginable creatures in the pitch-dark woods. Twigs and branches on the forest floor snapped and popped underfoot of unseen beasts, and the underbrush rustled all around in a light breeze. The Wyoming wilderness looked, sounded, felt, and even smelled different from anything I'd ever experienced.

"You would have loved this, Grandpa," I whispered quietly.

Most of the day had been spent driving from Utah through southern Idaho. I arrived in Yellowstone after dark, but found a suitable campsite near the lake in the heart of the park. Aided by the light of my new nickel-plated flashlight, I stomped down a flat place in a bed of pine needles about twenty-five feet from the water. Then I set out my bedroll. But before I settled in for the night, I went back to the truck and grabbed my grandfather's fishing hat, which I plopped on my head. Then I removed my mother's jewelry box from inside the dashboard.

I carried it to the edge of calm, massive Yellowstone Lake. Kneeling, I lifted the lid with care to find that the small amount of my grandfather's ashes I'd saved were still contained in the pewter box.

Slowly, I poured out the contents. In the reflection of the waning crescent moon I could see the gray dust swirling on the surface of the water for a moment. Then it coagulated, sank, and vanished.

PART TWO

22.

"NO KIDDING. Are you sure that's your old house, Hank?" asked Charlie Snyder, still holding the *Las Vegas Review-Journal* in front of my face. "I mean, couldn't that be any old foundation?"

"It's my home, without a doubt," I answered, gently pushing the newspaper away. "I don't care if it's been sixty years—I'd never forget what it looks like."

"Well, I'll be," he replied, stroking the white whiskers of his chin and taking a closer look at the photo. "So now what're you going to do? Do you think you might do a little visit up there?"

"Oh, I don't know about that," I said, standing up and fishing around in my hip pocket for my wallet. "It's possible. We'll see."

Perhaps it was the spirit of the holiday season, or maybe I was just feeling guilty about leaving my breakfast uneaten, but I pulled out a ten-dollar bill and dropped it on the table. The tab would have totaled less than five bucks, but I didn't care to wait around for it, and I was no longer hungry. It was rude to walk away from an untouched plate of food, but I hoped the generous tip would soothe the burn. The last thing I needed was to burn bridges at the Sahara Saloon. I ate about half my meals there.

"Well, Chuck, I have to get going," I said as I pushed in my seat and plucked my jacket from a coat hook. "I have some important things to take care of. You know, Christmas shopping and such. And I told my daughter I'd give her a call before eleven o'clock, so I do need to be on my way."

I patted him on the shoulder as I slipped by and shouted into the kitchen, "See you tomorrow, Louis. Sorry to run out!"

•

After a couple quick stops at a hardware store and my house, I hopped in my van and consulted an atlas. There were two options for driving from Vegas to St. Thomas. The quickest route would be to drive north on Interstate 15 to the Moapa exit, just past Glendale, and then head south on 169. Or I could head east from the city on Lake Mead Boulevard, traverse the pass between Frenchman and Sunrise Mountains, and hook onto Northshore Road, which meandered for fifty-five miles along Lake Mead.

I opted for the latter. While the Interstate would have saved time, it would've also required me to drive straight through Overton—and one blast from the past would suffice. Of course, by taking Northshore Road, I had to see the lake itself for the first time since I was twelve years old.

•

If a remorseless criminal had murdered my parents and burnt my home to the ground, I don't believe that the passage of any number of years would heal the wounds. He could rot in prison for decades and emerge old, wrinkled, and pathetic, and I'd still see a young and vicious outlaw.

So maybe that is how I'd have felt if I had come face to face with Hiram Johnson, Phil Swing, Calvin Coolidge, Walker Young, Elwood Mead, or any of the other long-deceased politicians, engineers, and bureaucrats who'd facilitated the construction of the dam and the creation of the lake. But as for the lake itself . . . now I flushed my toilet and brushed my teeth with its waters. Seeing it elicited neither ire nor sorrow.

It was striking how natural the lake now appeared to me, despite the abnormality of a sea plunked in an arid, drought-stricken desert. Even still, the sailboats delicately skimming across the sapphire lake just seemed to belong, as did the marinas and cultivated palm trees along the shore. The reddish backdrop of the mountainous Martian landscape made the deep blue tint of the water and sky seem even more dramatic.

Other than a few passing motorcycles, I was the only vehicle on the road. It wasn't unusual—beyond the city limits of Las Vegas and Henderson, the desert roads of southern Nevada are often lightly traveled and lonesome. Regardless, no amount of traffic would change the fact that loneliness had become the one constant in my life since the day my wife died more than five years earlier. Though I was on my way to my childhood home, it was toward her that my thoughts drifted.

I met Sarah the very first day I arrived at Eastern Montana State Normal School, only a day after releasing my grandfather's ashes into Yellowstone Lake. I encountered her walking across the school grounds not long after stepping out of my truck—and it's a moment I'll never forget. She was dressed in a white cashmere sweater and a navy blue skirt, and I could swear she looked just like a picture I might have seen once of a woman who I thought was possibly Ava Gardner. I couldn't be sure; we didn't have too many feature films or celebrity magazines in Overton.

I was as lost as a five-year-old wearing his sneakers on the wrong feet on his first day of kindergarten, but Sarah was kind enough to guide me around campus. Somehow, that chance meeting of a gorgeous young woman and a road-weary boy in stained, threadbare attire led to a romance that lasted more than five decades.

Sarah and I had a long, happy life together in Montana. We raised two beautiful children: John, born in 1956 and named for Sarah's father, and Ellen, born in 1962 and named for my mother. They'd given us three grandchildren all told. We were settling into old age just fine. We made grand plans to travel, just like Grandpa and I had many years before.

Yet once again, Death had other plans. Instead of a gentle and swift departure, Sarah's passing followed a punishing battle with cancer that stretched over nearly four excruciating years. I stayed with her while she fought it, often wishing that her suffering would end; yet when I said goodbye in August 1997, nearly fifty-three years to the day from our chance meeting, I realized that another fifty-three years together would not have been nearly enough.

I used to wonder: what is the ideal way to lose someone you love? Is it best to be there, right up to the end, standing by their side when they go? Or better to learn of their passing after the fact, from afar, where the reality of their death exists only in your mind, abstract and impalpable? Is it preferable to see it coming so that you can prepare for the inevitable, or is it better to be surprised by it so you don't waste a single shared moment of life worrying about or fighting against the things that you can't control anyway?

The answer is that there is no best way to say goodbye. When the time comes, when "she is" becomes "she was," the feeling is always the same.

Except for one thing: when my parents and grandfather passed, I wished I could bring them back. When Sarah died, I wished I could join her. Fall came, and then a long, bitter winter crawled by. There's not much more to say about it.

That spring I hit the road in a Westfalia and traveled the country alone. I spent four months on the road, like Steinbeck without Charley, and in September 1998 I bought the bungalow in Las Vegas. The idea of passing the summer months in the desert appealed none to me, but neither did spending another snowy winter alone in the Montana wilderness. I'd simply split my time between the two residences.

I hadn't chosen to winter in Nevada for nostalgic reasons. I simply wasn't drawn to any tropical destination, and the idea of loafing in some insular, golf course-lined senior citizen incubator like Boca Raton or Pebble Beach rather sickened me. Besides, it was out of my price range. Las Vegas merely seemed like a tolerable—and affordable—option.

Nevada was my birthplace and the state where I had spent my childhood years, but I'd become a Montanan through and through. By the time I purchased the Vegas house, I'd lived in the Treasure State for fifty-four years; as I drove toward St. Thomas, wishing more than anything that Sarah were seated beside me, I contemplated just how swiftly those years had passed by.

•

The hour-long drive passed quickly. Then, suddenly, forking off to the right from the smooth blacktop was the Old St. Thomas Road. I turned onto it and began the rough-and-tumble final stretch.

After a few miles, the washed-out dirt road came to a dead end at the top of a small plateau. I stepped out of my van and gauged my location—I was parked just north of where Grandpa and I had landed our boat on June 11, 1938, shortly after he'd set the house afire. At the edge of the plateau, a short, steep bank led to the lowlands of the valley. Unlike the rust-red desert I'd driven through, which teemed with plant life in spite of its aridity, the valley floor was dead and black, coated with cracked, tacky mud where the lake bottom had been only months earlier. About a half-mile to the south I spotted the edge of the receding Lake Mead shoreline.

And inland from the shore less than a hundred yards . . . home.

At least, what was left of it. From my vantage point I could see little more than small fragments of concrete jutting up from the slime, reaching out of the muck like the outstretched arms of skeletons. Clearly, the corpse of St. Thomas had been exhumed.

My mouth was dry, but it wasn't from thirst. The day suddenly felt gloomy and cold despite the beaming sun and the uncommonly warm December weather. For more than sixty years I had imagined what it would be like to return home, but now that I was here, I felt compelled to jump back behind the wheel and flee. Instead, I went around to the rear of my vehicle, took out my heavy knapsack, and lifted it onto my back. It was loaded with every tool I could think of that might help me crack open a rusted, mud-caked safe like a nut. I'd bought a claw hammer, an iron mallet, a garden spade, a cat's paw, and a crowbar, plus a flashlight and two large bottles of water—one for drinking and one for washing away dirt.

I locked up the vehicle and shot a furtive glance over my shoulder to make sure that no park ranger was sneaking up behind me. No, I was not being followed or watched. I skidded down the dusty bank and began the muddy, mile-long hike into town.

•

Most people who return home after years away find subtle changes. Their favorite bookstore has gone out of business, or a shopping plaza has sprung up in what used to be a swamp. These transformations are small potatoes when compared to watching your village sink like Atlantis, only to surface like a whale carcass more than half a century later.

Perhaps that's too generous a metaphor though. St. Thomas's carcass had been stripped clean by the federal vultures in the 1930s, and only its bones were left to drown.

Stumps of trees that had been dead longer than they were allowed to live lined the Arrowhead Trail highway, the imprint of which still bisected the town from east to west. Twisted wooden fenceposts marked forgotten property lines, and building foundations peeked through silt and mud. I looked to the right and saw the footprint of the hotel, a brick-lined path still leading up to its invisible front door. Down the road sat the concrete pad where the pool hall had once been, and farther in the distance were the remnants of Hannig's Ice Cream Parlor. Its chimney still stood, the highest remaining structure in the entire ghost town.

If there is such a thing as a "ghost lake," then St. Thomas fit that bill too. Thousands of white fresh-water mussel shells littered the valley and crunched beneath the soles of my boots with every step. Sixty years' worth of lost boat anchors and cables lay scattered about, half-sunken into the desert floor.

Some things hadn't changed though. All the hills and mountains lining the horizon remained unmoved and unaltered. What are sixty years to a multimillion-year-old range but a meaningless drop in an eternal ocean of time? Virgin Peak still loomed, tall and verdant, watching with infinite patience the futile transformations in the Moapa wasteland. It knew, even if we didn't, that eventually the desert would reclaim what we tried to take. You can build on it, and you can flood it out, but someday it will all return to sand and saltbush.

As I contemplated this thought, I shuffled down the road with my neck bent, staring at my feet so I wouldn't trip or slip in the mud and fall to my doom. Break a hip out in a lonesome desert, and it's likely you won't be found until you're nothing but a shriv-eled-up mummy in hiking gear. Instinct guided me along. When I looked up, I was standing in my old front yard.

A dozen times or more I circled the protrud-ing concrete foundation. It was far smaller than I'd remembered. How had our living room, kitchen, and dining area fit into this minuscule square space?

In the back of the house, a rusted grate covered the old cistern. I looked down into the brackish liquid and saw my reflection, covered in part by a dead snake bobbing in the sludge. Standing by where the back door had been, I tried to envision my grandfather stepping out into his dinghy and shoving off to search for my mother. It was almost impossible to see it though. My mind was like a television with busted rabbit ears and lousy reception—I tried to make out a clear image, but everything was static and fuzz. This was the place; I knew that without question. Yet I still couldn't visualize how it had been.

That is, until I took a good, long look at the foundation window opening.

My heart pounded so hard and so rapidly that I was afraid I might keel over and die of a heart attack right then and there. I slouched at the waist and placed a hand on the edge of the foundation, right where a bit of rebar poked through, and caught my breath. When my breathing slowed, I slipped off the backpack and dropped it to the ground. It was a relief to release that massive weight.

Taking care not to strain my aching knees or back, I gradually lowered myself and kneeled by the opening of the window. Then I removed my flashlight from the bag and stuck my head into the hole.

There it was: the one part of St. Thomas most unchanged since my youth. Instead of fine silt on the floor I found hard, cracked, clay, and the windowpanes had been punched out by the pressure of more than seventy feet of water. But it was otherwise the same: dark, cool, quiet, and cramped.

I shined the flashlight into the small cavern. An old habit returned, and I swept the beam from wall to wall, looking for spiders and rattlers, just like Dad had taught me. It was clean. Then I shook off the nostalgia and remembered my mission. I blasted the far wall with light, and sure enough, partly buried in the earth but still recognizable, clear as I remembered it, sat the old Mosler safe.

•

The space that had seemed small when I was a child was even tighter now. Over time, sludgy sand had drifted in and shrunk the gap from dirt to concrete to less than three feet, and I had to shimmy flat on my belly in places where the gap was smallest. I held the flashlight out in front and dragged the backpack behind me, slithering like a snake in the mud. A minute later I reached the safe.

While it was chilly in the crawlspace, sweat gushed from my forehead and streamed into my eyes. But with a film of black dirt coating my fingers and arms, I couldn't wipe it away. No matter—I'd dig out the safe and have it open in no time. There was no telling what condition it was in—let alone the condition of the contents it held—but I had to at least find out. I thought of my father and the feeling of guilt I'd had when the lake water rushed in, stealing my chance to rescue his prized belongings that he'd asked me to save if anything should happen to him. Now I'd make good on a nearly seventy-year-old promise.

Lying flat on my belly, I reached back and rummaged blindly in the sack for the garden spade. Once I got my hand on it and fished it out of the bag, I propped myself up on my left elbow and began to dig furiously in front of the heavy steel-and-iron box.

White blisters began to form on the soft, wrinkled skin of my hand, but they slowed me down none, and within minutes I'd excavated several inches of soil along the length of the safe, creating a small space for the door to open—not all the way, but enough so that I could reach my hand inside.

The next step was to try getting into the safe the easy way: by using the combination lock. But first, I needed a drink of water in the worst way. If I'd thought I was sweating before, the act of vigorously scooping out thick, partially dried lake-bottom mud had caused gallons of perspiration to erupt from the pores of my body. My nervousness wasn't helping any either.

I uncapped one of the bottles and drank deep, tilting my head to the side and awkwardly taking big gulps from the corner of my mouth. After downing my fill, I poured a small amount of water over the dial to rinse away the dirt crust. Then I set the bottle down an arm's length away without capping it.

"To open this safe, you have to remember three numbers. And it should be pretty easy because the numbers are your birthday: 8, 20, 26."

Now I was having some clear memories. Under the

house where little had changed since my childhood, I could hear my father's instructions as if he were right there beside me, gently guiding me.

I gripped the dial to give it a spin—but nothing happened. The dial was lodged in place, and no matter how hard I tried to force it, it would not budge. Whatever amount of strength was needed to turn the combination lock, I did not possess it.

Over the next twenty minutes, I broke out nearly every tool in my arsenal. I tapped the dial with the hammer, hoping to jar it loose, but it remained stuck. With that having failed, I flipped the hammer around and tried to wedge the claw into the small gap of the safe door, hoping to pry it open, but the claw would not fit. So I slid the flat chisel end of the cat's paw into the door crack, and once it was firmly in place I rapped the opposite end with the mallet, using it like a lever. However, after only four whacks the tool was bent out of shape. The door remained tightly sealed.

My patience was waning, and dismay was beginning to creep over me. Why had I been so hasty to rush out here? Why hadn't I taken the time to read up on safes? For more than sixty years I'd been a scholar, yet in one of the biggest moments of my life I'd failed to take any time whatsoever to educate myself on how safes work, how to break into one if a lock fails, and whether they were even waterproof. I didn't know if the contents, whatever they may be, had remained dry for all these years. For all I knew, the coffer contained nothing but photos and banknotes that had been reduced to slurry in 1938. All this struggle for what could essentially be an empty box.

Unfortunately, my good sense had been compromised by the possibility that something *was* still in there and that I'd be able to retrieve it. Excitement in, common sense out. Seventy-six years old and I still hadn't learned to always be prepared, nor to always expect the worst.

By this time I'd been under the house in the mud for far too long. My chest, stomach, and thighs ached from being pressed into the ground, and my neck and shoulders burned. Blisters had torn open on my hands. I was too old for this, and I badly wanted to crawl out of the claustrophobic space. However, I had one last instrument in my bag, and I wasn't going to leave until I'd tried everything.

"You can do this," I whispered to myself as I removed the heavy crowbar from the backpack. Deception isn't my strong suit; I've never been a good liar. I knew I couldn't do this. Regardless, I took a deep breath, tightened my grip with both hands, and slashed away at the safe.

With so little space from floor to ceiling, it was difficult to get any leverage on the bar. Still, I hit the safe hard. I smacked the side of the box, hoping it would break open like a walnut; I hammered the dial, trying to free it from whatever corrosion had rendered it immovable; I jabbed at the gap in the door, trying to pop it ajar. While I flailed, the crowbar scraped the underside of the concrete above and dug into the earth below. As I inadvertently dug little holes, clods of dirt flew all around, covering my backside and binding to my sticky, sweat-soaked flesh. Finally, after dozens of pointless stabs at the safe door, I gave up and dropped the instrument off to the side.

Thunk.

The heavy bar knocked into my aluminum water bottle. I craned my neck and shined the flashlight to see the bottle, tipped over, emptying the last of its contents into a small pit near my waist that I'd unintentionally gouged with the end of my crowbar.

Though I was a short walk from an enormous freshwater lake, the sight of seeing a spilled bottle of liquid in the desert caused me to panic reflexively. I spun around like a crab and grabbed the bottle, setting it upright just as the last drop of water fell out into the wet soil.

Something in the shallow hole caught my eye. I stretched out my left arm to retrieve the flashlight, and then shined the beam into the excavated area that was now just beneath my chin. The water had washed the dirt from an object that looked similar to the white shells littering the desert floor—but though I'd seen plenty of shells surrounding the foundation of the house, I hadn't seen any *under* it. Just this one, and it was buried below an inch or more of firm sediment.

I dug in with my fingertips, pulling away small chunks of soil. The mysterious sea creature had been fairly large—I'd unearthed about six inches of the pale, porous shell, and it appeared to keep going. It was long but narrow, and appeared to be partially dissolved. Whatever it was, it had been down here for some time.

Then, surprisingly, as I chipped away, another bright color glinted in the mud. I pointed the flashlight at the shimmering yellow speck and raked the dirt away from it. It came loose from the mud and I pulled it out. Dangling from my fingertips was a thin gold chain with a tarnished golden locket attached.

It was so improbable that recognition came on slowly, and when it did, I momentarily rejected the idea. But there it was, and it was undeniable. It was the locket and chain that had belonged to my mother. She always wore it.

This was no sea creature I was digging up—it was the remnants of her skeleton.

I couldn't breathe, couldn't blink. The necklace quivered and danced as it drooped from my trembling hand. Then it slipped from my fingers as a sudden, guttural shriek escaped my mouth, amplified as loud as a fire siren by the close confines of the concrete: "*Yee-eee!*" It was a sound I'd never before made during my nearly eighty years. I scrambled backward, dropping the light, and as I tried to squeeze my way out of the opening, I cracked the back of my skull on the rough cement edge of the window and knocked myself unconscious.

23.

I T WASN'T LONG before I came to. As I lifted my cheek off the ground I felt sick, confused, and frightened. When I was young, I never would have thought that an old man could feel this way, so much like a child.

I was also incredibly thirsty, and my remaining bottle of water—as well as the rest of my stuff—was spread all throughout the crawlspace. Sighing, I resigned myself to what must be done and shimmied back under the house. The shock had worn off, but I still wasn't comfortable down there. It was like crawling into my own mother's coffin.

Now I understood that she too had known about the safe all along. It wasn't a secret between me and my dad—that was just something I'd imagined because I had been a child. Of *course* my mother knew. When the downpour began on that evening in 1938, it became apparent to her that the deluge would soon make the safe permanently inaccessible. Panicking, she raced out into the storm in the dark and crawled beneath the house to rescue the valuables.

But the flood moved in too quickly. The crawl-space filled and she wasn't able to make her escape. While Grandpa and I were out in the boat trying to make it home, Mom was drowning under the pantry. Her body had been there all along, just beneath our feet.

•

Later, after gathering my tools, bottles, and bag, I located the foundation of my grandfather's old garage. The grease pit was still there, though it was completely filled in with sediment. I stared blankly at it for a minute or two and then found my way to the ruins of the St. Thomas School, which had been torn down just before the flood. All that remained were the front steps, a pair of collapsed support columns, and a massive, empty foundation hole where the building once stood. Unlike my house, it seemed to occupy a much larger space than I'd remembered.

It now was late afternoon, and being so close to the winter solstice, the sun had already started to set. With a throbbing headache and an aching body, coated in filth from head to toe, I began to limp in the direction of the truck. I'd seen all I needed to see for now.

There would be other days to seek out more pieces of the puzzle of my past. As I hobbled through the rapidly darkening valley, I knew without question that in spite of the events of the day, I would be back. The safe remained sealed, and I still had a promise to keep. In the meantime, there was much research to be done. Books to read, experts to consult, more tools to purchase. The next time I arrived in St. Thomas, I'd be prepared to crack open the safe my mother had died trying to unlock. Otherwise, I'd haul it out of the valley, even if I had to drag it out inch by inch.

My mother, however, would stay put. If someone were to argue that her remains deserved to be given a proper burial, I wouldn't disagree. But to me, it makes sense that she should be there beneath the remnants of her home. Her parents and sister had burned to death, and their ashes had never left St. Thomas. Grandma Lord lay beneath the site of the former town graveyard, and my father, though he was buried on higher ground, had died in the water. Grandpa died in Overton, but his cremated body was scattered in the lake to settle on the land he'd loved. The remains of my family were together to rest with the remains of their hometown. There was some odd comfort in that.

Eventually, all traces of them will vanish entirely, as will the lake and the ruins of St. Thomas. You can build on it, and you can flood it out, but someday the Moapa Valley and everything in it will return to sand and saltbush. Someday I will go too, to join all those Lords who've passed before me. It may not be imminent, but it is inevitable. I'm an old man; most days I'm not even sure why I am still here or why the die-rolls of destiny have landed in favor of my survival for so long.

They certainly didn't favor my wife, who suffered tremendously and departed full of tubes and tumors in a hospital bed. They didn't favor most of my grand-parents, nor my dad and mom, who both died so young and in such horrible ways. Think about it: my mom lost her mother, her father, her sister, her hus-band, her home, and her career, and yet fate still saw to it that she wouldn't live to see her only child reach his twelfth birthday.

Even in the desert, some people drown. Others survive just long enough to tell about it. Somehow, I am still here.

Remains of the Fenton Whitney Home, inspiration for Henry Lord's home.

Garage pit (filled in) at the remains of Hugh Lord's Garage.
Photos taken by Jackson Ellis, November 4, 2012.

ABOUT THE AUTHOR

JACKSON ELLIS is a writer and editor from Vermont who has also spent time living in Nevada and Montana. His short fiction has appeared in *The Vermont Literary Review, Sheepshead Review, Broken Pencil, The Birmingham Arts Journal, East Coast Literary Review, Midwest Literary Magazine,* and *The Journal of Microliterature.* He is the co-publisher of *Verbicide* magazine, which he founded in 1999. *Lords of St. Thomas* was his first book. His second book, *Black Days,* came out in 2024,

A NOTE ON THE TYPE

Lords of St. Thomas was typeset in Minion. In designing Minion font, Robert Slimbach was inspired by the timeless beauty of the fonts of the late Renaissance. Minion was created primarily as a traditional text font but adapts well to today's digital technology, presenting the richness of the late baroque forms within modern text formats. This clear, balanced font is suitable for almost any use. The inspiration for Slimbach's design came from late Renaissance period classic typefaces in the old serif style. The Renaissance period was noted for its elegant and attractive typefaces that were also highly readable. The name Minion is derived from the traditional classification and naming of typeface sizes, minion being a size in between brevier and nonpareil. It approximates to a modern 7 point lettering size. The Minion design's lowercase characters use old-style glyphs in keeping with its Baroque typeface roots. These are most noticeable on the lowercase "g" and "q." Subtle, but important, details allow the upper and lower case to match well and sit comfortably next to each other. The letter "z" in both cases has the tell-tale heavy dropped serif and matching line thicknesses. The strokes of the upper and lower case "y", with its italicized narrowing of the secondary stroke, reinforce the strength of the primary stroke. Interestingly, the "Z" character has a thick stroke in perpendicularity to the "Y," and though it may look a little odd on close examination, within a body of text it enhances readability by providing good differentiation between adjacent letters. The overall appearance of the Minion design is very much related to the appearance of mass-produced publications of late Renaissance but there is an added touch of classic typography design not possible with older, inaccurate print machinery. This new take on those old styles has produced a crisper outline. The Minion typeface family has been expertly crafted to retain great readability by producing a print clarity that even the best of the Renaissance typographers could not manage.

•

TEXT DESIGN BY DEDE CUMMINGS

COVER DESIGN & ILLUSTRATION BY NATHANIEL POLLARD